THE SPIDER:
THE CHOLERA KING

THE CHOLERA KING

By Grant Stockbridge

STEEGER BOOKS • 2020

CHAPTER 1
THE BLACK CROSS

R ICHARD WENTWORTH'S high forehead was marked by a frown as he stood at the aft rail of the *S. S. Bremen*, a forty-five caliber automatic in each hand. He told himself sharply that he was foolish to be suspicious of a man who had challenged him to this shooting match. His constant need for alertness against bitter, ever-present enemies was making him overly cautious… But the uneasy feeling persisted. A shooting match compelled him to turn his back on a man he did not know—a man who was holding a loaded gun in his hand!

A clay pigeon arched out from the lower deck where a steward was operating the traps. Wentworth's right hand gun blasted from the hip. The target smashed, rained fragments down upon the frothing wake of the ship… Of course, Nita van Sloan was behind him too. She could watch the man, but she was unarmed, and it had seemed foolish to warn her… A second target skittered to the left and his other gun shattered that. He turned and smiled at the man who had challenged, glanced toward Nita….

"You see why I disliked to accept your wager," he said to the man, whose name was Frank Hoffman.

Hoffman was young, with a high mass of curly, blond hair. He had a hearty laugh… But somehow, this time, his laughter

did not ring quite true. "You're good," Hoffman conceded, "but my chance is coming…."

Nita van Sloan called out sharply, "Dick!"

Wentworth whipped about, snapped a shot at a target which had almost reached the sea. Its fragments made a little circle of splashes. He did not look about again, but stood relaxed, guns hanging at his sides. When a target offered, he automatically

2

Thousands of scenes like this were being enacted all over the city!

lifted the weapon nearest the pigeon… His thoughts were not on his shooting.

They did not have to be, even though he was giving a really remarkable demonstration of target work. Men usually fired at this type of target with shotguns, aiming carefully, following the target with the muzzle. Wentworth was snap-shooting….

He had always maintained that there was nothing remarkable about his accuracy, that any man who gave it the same amount of time—who had had to depend on his guns for his life, as Wentworth had—would develop the same ability. He had practiced tirelessly and his guns had stood him in good stead on many a perilous campaign against the Underworld, to the suppression of which he had pledged his life….

Subconsciously, he counted the shots, *four, five…* He carried seven in each gun, one in the barrel chamber, six in the clip. Impatiently, he dismissed his suspicions of Hoffman… There was a black speck there on the horizon, where the setting sun gleamed like a sullen fire. The speck was too large, too steady in its flight to be a seabird. But what would a plane be doing out here, so many miles from the shore? There were no transatlantic flights under way… *Six.* That left one bullet in the right gun, three in the left. He used the left one on the next target… That speck *was* a plane, approaching very rapidly… *Six.* That left one bullet in the left hand gun also….

Behind trim, Nita van Sloan screamed an abrupt warning. "Dick, *look out!*"

WENTWORTH DID not whirl as most men would have done to see the cause for that scream. He relaxed all the muscles of his body and spilled himself prone. While he was still falling, a gun barked, kept on barking, behind him. He hit the deck, rolled, his own guns coming up. Hoffman was crouched, his young face savage, his lips twisted to bare his teeth. Three shots had sped from his gun, cutting just above Wentworth. As he fell, a fourth bullet whanged on the steel mesh below the railing....

Wentworth steadied his right hand gun coolly—his left arm was pinned awkwardly beneath him—and squeezed the trigger... A cry burst from his lips. Across the line of fire, a woman had flung herself, straight toward Hoffman's gun. It was Nita!

Something like a sob drove up through Wentworth's throat. He tried to jerk up the muzzle of his gun, hurled himself to his feet the same instant, his eyes never leaving the tableau before him. Because of his split-second control of his muscles, he had been able to throw his bullet over Nita's head, but that gun was now empty! It would take precious moments to have his left gun ready to shoot... Nita van Sloan had seized Hoffman's gun wrist with her left hand. With her right, the first two fingers pronged and stiffened, she was striking at his eyes and throat. If she could hit certain nerve centers there....

Hoffman spun and wrenched, trying to rip the gun from Nita's grasp. Her feet were snapped clear of the floor and she fell heavily to her knees, but still she clung to the gun. Hoffman's glance shot beyond her to Wentworth, saw him half off the floor, his left hand automatic rising. The man's eyes flared wide as he looked into Wentworth's implacable gaze. With a hoarse scream, he abandoned struggling for the gun in Nita's hands, sprang for the rail and poised a scant moment on its top. Then he arched out into space, plunging toward the water. Wentworth was back on his feet now. He could smash a bullet into Hoffman's body before the assassin hit the water, but he held his fire. The man could not escape now. And if he could be rescued from the sea, it might be possible to force some explanation from him....

Wentworth lifted Nita to her feet, put an arm about her waist, took her to the railing and watched Hoffman's head bobbing as the wake from the propellers battered him. Nita was sobbing with anger.

"Damn him," she whispered. "Damn him, Dick, he... he almost... He...!"

"Shhh, darling," Wentworth whispered. "Shhh! He did, but you saved my life..." He could feel the rigidity of her body under his arm. Cords stood out beneath the soft skin of her throat. "I—I couldn't reach his throat," she said, "and he hurt my knees."

Wentworth laughed and squeezed her. An officer was racing aft along the deck, shouting inquiries in guttural English. The ship's whistle belched a deep note and someone shouted, "Man overboard!"

Abruptly, Wentworth stiffened, jerked his eyes toward the sky. The plane! It had come up rapidly and was circling; no more man a half-mile astern there, dipping toward the water.

Damn it, this had all been carefully planned. Hoffman's leap overboard had been part of the scheme, and that airplane back there was here in mid-Atlantic to pick him up! He half-whirled to urge the ship's officer to speed back, but he knew it was useless. The *Bremen's* 28-knot pace had left Hoffman far behind and the plane was already on the surface. They'd have the assassin aboard and be gone again before the *Bremen* could complete its turn....

THE OFFICER was beside them now, still shouting. "You

can proceed on your way," Wentworth told him shortly. "A man
attempted to assassinate me and
leaped overboard. He has already
been rescued by a confederate in
that plane. Will you use your glasses,
please, and see if you can read its
numbers?"

The officer cried, "Assassin? You're mad… mad…!" He turned
to Wentworth, met the impact of his gray-blue gaze and abruptly
subsided, his face growing dark with embarrassment. He clicked
his heels, bowed stiffly. "Your pardon, sir," he mumbled thickly,
"but you must admit it is startling."

Wentworth said impatiently, "All right, all right! Use your
glasses and get the plane's number."

The plane was already wheeling for a take-off; Hoffman was
clambering up from a pontoon to a wing and the cockpit. The
officer trained his glasses on the ship, shook his head. Impatiently, Wentworth took the binoculars, but it was clearly useless.
Either the seaplane's numbers had been painted out or there was
some means of covering them temporarily….

Moments later, the craft bounced into the air and circled
slowly upward. There was a soft step on the deck beside Wentworth and he glanced about, smiled slightly as he met the
anxious eyes of a powerfully built Hindu who wore a white
turban bound tightly about his head and whose full, bushy beard
could not hide the alarm on his swarthy face.

"I heard shouting, master," he said, his nasal voice harsh in his native Punjabi dialect. He was a Sikh, a member of the most warlike tribe of India.

Wentworth handed him the two empty automatics. "Fresh clips, Ram Singh," he ordered. And then: "One attempted my life and is fleeing in that airplane."

The Sikh's bearded lips smiled back from his white teeth. *"Wah, sahib!* There is a small plane in the bows, that which brought the mail. Thy servant could fly after him...."

Wentworth's eyes gleamed, then he shook his head, laughed shortly. Ram Singh referred to the catapult plane which had flown to the ship with the late mail yesterday evening. It was lashed to the deck, and could be quickly released, but it would not have the speed necessary to overtake that ship ahead. He gave his arm to Nita, led her toward the suite she shared with the gray-haired dowager, Mrs. Robinson, whom Wentworth employed as a companion for her on the rare occasions when they could travel together....

"Do thou stand, ever at my back, Ram Singh," he said briefly to the Sikh, speaking in Punjabi also. They advanced rapidly along the decks... Wentworth said little even in the suite as a stewardess dressed the abrasions on Nita's knees. He paced with long, lithe strides up and down the main salon, went out on the

Richard Wentworth

private deck and stared out over the brazen surface of the water, his thoughts turbulent.

DEAR NITA. Her bravery was a match for his own. Well he knew that if she could have stopped those bullets no other way, she would have stopped their tearing death with her own sweet body. Damn it, what was behind this new attack upon him? He had no more than a month ago put down a fierce uprising of the Underworld, had nearly lost his life in the fight. Now he was bound abroad for a short rest, a peaceful time with Nita. It seemed his enemies did not will him to rest!

Wentworth clasped his lean hands, leaned his forearms on the railing. Was it possible that someone bad discovered his secret identity? Did some new master-criminal aspire to organize the Underworld and seek to pave the way by murdering… the Spider?

That was the personality Wentworth had created to carry his justice to criminals—a stooped, caped figure who went silently and terribly through the night, bringing his dread judgment to those the police could not reach, leaving on their chilling foreheads the small, crimson seal of his wrath, a glistening spider….

Yet, it was not necessarily true that they had learned who he was. In his own identity, Richard Wentworth was an amateur criminologist, a close friend of the Commissioner of Police, a man whom the authorities often consulted in time of stress. He had fought powerfully in that way, too, against the criminals, had created a host of bitter enemies….

His finely chiseled lips clamped firmly together. His duty was plain. He must speed back to New York and seek out the reason for this new attack. Damnable that it should spoil this rare outing with Nita. She would not complain, God knew, but….

Wentworth's head whipped up sharply. A shadow had fallen across the ship… He stared out into the red fury of the evening sky, saw the plane on which Hoffman was making his escape. It seemed almost motionless against the sun, a black cross in the heavens, the black shadow of that cross smudging the ship's high side. Wentworth frowned. The thing was strangely sinister, an evil portent in this night of trouble....

Good God, *what was that?* Up on a higher deck, a man had uttered a shrill scream of pain and terror! The sound rolled on and on, sobbing into the twilight, strangling, horrible. With a muffled curse, Wentworth darted across Nita's salon. She had jerked to her feet. The stewardess knelt bolt upright on the floor and there was a fearful question in the two women's eyes.

"Stay here!" Wentworth called, as he sped into the corridor. "God knows what has happened now!"

As he hurried to a companionway, he was aware of Ram Singh hard on his heels. He took his reloaded automatics from the Sikh, then dashed up steep stairs, swung out on the deck. Frightened men and women were hurrying away from the spot where the scream had sounded. Wentworth fought the human tide, came presently to a man who lay writhing upon the deck. He was bent double over his folded arms, his limbs rigid, his breath hoarse in his throat. A steward was kneeling beside him; another ran for the ship's surgeon....

Wentworth stood staring down at the crumpled figure for a long moment. He heard a harsh Punjab oath grate in Ram Singh's throat, felt the Sikh's hand upon his arm.

"*Sahib!*" Ram Singh whispered. "In the name of the All High, *sahib*, come away!"

Wentworth frowned. "What's the matter, Ram Singh?"

"Don't you remember, *sahib?*" the Sikh said quickly, still

tugging insistently at Wentworth's arm. "That summer in Bengal, with men dropping like flies in the streets!"

A GASP burned Wentworth's throat. He stared at the writhing man, then jerked the steward away violently.

"Keep away from him, man," he commanded harshly. "Go wash your hands—your whole body—with germicidal soap. Throw your clothing overboard, or better still, burn it."

The steward stared at Wentworth with bulging eyes. "In heaven's name," he whispered, "what... what do you mean, sir?"

Wentworth stood staring with pitying gaze at the man on the deck. The victim was entirely conscious; his eyes looked beseechingly at them, while his body still twitched with pain. Wentworth had seen other men lie thus in the streets of Bengal towns, had seen their faces turn wrinkled and old before his eyes, had seen the violet tinge of death creep over their faces and limbs which twitched with perpetual convulsions. God, he should recognize the most dread plague of India, the scourge which killed thousands every year and had swept the wide world in five or six great epidemics to pile the dead in droves upon the sidewalks—men dying too swiftly for the survivors to destroy the death-spreading cadavers.

"Please, sir," whispered the steward, "what do you mean? Your face... You frighten me!"

Wentworth laughed shortly. "I frighten myself," he said. "If this is the epidemic variety..." He shut his lips into a thin gash. "Do as I told you."

The surgeon arrived hurriedly, dropped down beside the dying man; his ruddy cheeks abruptly paled. "A stretcher, quickly, steward!" he snapped. The surgeon rose slowly as the men ran off and he met Wentworth's grim gaze.

"You… *know!*" he whispered.

Wentworth nodded slowly. "You'll make microscopic tests at once, of course," he said quietly. "If this is the Asiatic variety of cholera…."

"Yes, yes!" the surgeon agreed hurriedly. "But how could it be? How could it…?"

The man on the deck writhed in a new convulsion, bent double with the violence of his nausea. When at last it was over, the surgeon whipped open his case, took a pill from a vial and forced it through the man's blue-tinged lips.

"Calomel," the surgeon explained huskily. "It has been known to help even in Asiatic cholera. For God's sake, keep this quiet, sir!"

The frightened stewards returned and lifted the man to a stretcher, hurried him to the sick bay. The surgeon followed, his choppy strides making his rotund body bob erratically.

"It *is* the cholera of India, *sahib!*" Ram Singh whispered confidently. "I have seen it far too often…."

Wentworth turned, thin-lipped, to the railing. The plane still hung there against the sullen sunset. The ominous black cross of its shadow was heavy on the ship….

CHAPTER 2
CATAPULT

IT HAD been nearly eight o'clock when Hoffman made his cowardly attempt on Wentworth's life. It was nearly midnight when the surgeon sent for him, summoned him from where he sat with Nita on the promenade deck. At Wentworth's suggestion, the ship's water supply had been padlocked immediately after the man was seized with cholera on the deck....

Nita insisted on going with Wentworth to the captain's office and, despite the threat of ghastly peril, they seemed gay as they strolled along the deck, Wentworth tall in formal clothing, Nita in the rich blue she wore so well, a silken scarf about her exquisite shoulders. Kings could have no prouder bearing than Wentworth; the strong shoulders erect and confident, the carriage of the head a little arrogant with its crisp black crown of hair. And Nita was a fit companion, a queen....

Wentworth knocked lightly on the door of the captain's office, stepped in... and knew the message he had been summoned to hear. He read it in the grim set of the captain's jaw, in the paleness that painted gray on the ruddy cheeks of the surgeon....

"The *spirilla* are there," the doctor announced, his voice thin and high, "the comma *bacilli* of Koch. The patient is dying and the calomel cure does not work. Almost constant cramps over the entire body. In another hour...."

Wentworth's lips were drawn thinly together. He nodded. It was, as he had feared, the Asiatic cholera. It was a fearful disease, more swift and almost as deadly as the bubonic plague, the Black Death of the Middle Ages. It was usually spread through the water supply, and its period of incubation in the human body varied from a few hours to a day or two at most. Within five hours after seizure, the victim might die. If he lasted through forty-eight hours of the virulent cholera, he would probably recover. But less than a third of all those stricken would  survive that second day! Seven out of every ten persons taken ill would surely die!

A steward beat frenziedly on the door, rushed in without permission. *"Herr Doktor!"* he cried in guttural German. "On the promenade deck, a *Fräulein…!"* The surgeon came to his feet swiftly, but with a hopelessness that showed in his drooping shoulders. He glanced at Wentworth as he passed, said wearily: "I was afraid of this, afraid… That man…."

Wentworth knew what he meant. The man had been one of those in whom the germs had incubated swiftly. Even though the water supply was cut off and the ship was supplying beers and wines to take its place, there might still be seizures during the next forty-eight hours from previous infections….

A cold anger coursed through Wentworth's veins. It was a queer coincidence that the attack upon himself, and the black shadowy cross should herald so closely the first onslaught of the cholera! In what natural way could the cholera have broken out on the ship, or the water supply have become contaminated?

Wentworth felt that he knew the answer, though he shrank from accepting the theory. Before this, human monsters had loosed plagues on humanity to further personal ambitions!

Nita's hand was gripping his arm. He covered it with his own, turned to meet the captain's steady gaze.

"I am proceeding under forced draft," the commander announced heavily. "From England, a plane to us with serum will fly. But I am afraid it will be too late. I hope that in your country, they will be able the epidemic to stop...."

Wentworth took a tense step forward. "In America!" he cried. "Do you mean that there has been an outbreak there?"

THE CAPTAIN'S large head nodded slowly. "*Ach,* I had forgotten it was not on the bulletin board. *Ja,* in New York, tonight, seventy-five cases are taken to the hospital, already."

Wentworth whirled to face Nita. Her smile, despite the pallor of her face, was brave. "Yes, Dick," she said, "you'll have to go. And I'm going with you!"

He clasped her hands. "No, dear," he objected, "you can't go back into that. New York will be a pest-house within a week, if what I suspect is true. You can't...."

Nita's chin lifted. "Dick," she said quietly, "for months now you haven't let me help you. You've run all the risks alone. It's selfish, and I won't submit. *I'm going with you!*"

Wentworth caught her shoulders in his hands and shook her slightly. He turned to the captain.

"I want to commandeer your catapult plane," he declared firmly. "I'm going back to New York. They'll be needing me there."

The captain's blue eyes widened a little. "I can't do that, Mr. Wentworth," he demurred gravely. "You forget that the ship is under quarantine! That's enough to make it *verboten*. Besides, it would be suicide…."

Wentworth smiled quietly. He had expected that, and he was prepared. He bowed with a click of his heels, and excused himself. Nita hurried along beside him….

"Dick, I'm going with you!"

"The catapult plane only carries one," he reminded her gravely. "But quite aside from that…."

"You'd leave me here on this pest ship!"

They had reached Nita's suite. Wentworth shut the door behind them, took her close in his arms and looked down into the violet depths of her eyes.

"Dear," he said, "if either you or I have already been infected with the germs, neither staying here nor going ashore will help. The ship's water supply is cut off, so that there is no further danger of infection if you are careful. You will be much safer on this ship, and in England or Europe, than in New York."

"It isn't," Nita pointed out stubbornly, "that I'm interested in safety. You're going back to New York, so I'm going too. We won't argue about it any more."

She stepped away from him smiling. "If you'll leave now, Mr. Wentworth, I'll get dressed for the trip."

Wentworth gazed at her steadily through a long moment, a small answering smile on his lips. Damnable to love each other as they did, and yet to live a fruitless, barren life. They could never marry. A man with the hourly threat of the law—of death at enemy hands—over his head could not have a home and wife and children. He had explained all that to Nita long ago when their love had proved too strong for the will Wentworth had set against it. His life had already been dedicated to the ceaseless crusade of keeping criminal hordes from the throat of humanity. He could not swerve from the service he had chosen, nor would Nita have had him do so. But she insisted upon the right to share his life and his constant danger. For long months, they had fought side by side, but time after time, the Spider's enemies had struck at him through his love until now he felt he no longer had the right to imperil her....

Yet it was bitter to deny her and himself the boon of shared danger. He laughed softly, gathered her in his arms again before he went to the door....

"I'LL BE ready in ten minutes," Nita called blithely as Wentworth strode away. She would be hurt when she found he had left her—but he could not take her. He would not....

In his quarters, he flung swift orders at Ram Singh. The Sikh's teeth flashed through his beard. He took a gun from a suitcase, thrust it into the sash which belted his tunic and stepped silently from the stateroom. Wentworth caught up a topcoat, threw a kiss at a portrait of Nita hanging on the wall, and went swiftly down the corridor. When Nita's ten minutes had elapsed, he would already be in the air, speeding westward....

When he reached the forward deck, a half-dozen seamen were busy casting off the lashings of the ship, which had been placed upon the catapult boom. Ram Singh stood beside a young officer and the nine-inch blade of his knife was pricking the seaman's loins just above the kidney... Wentworth paused beside them.

"I am sorry about this," he apologized quietly, "but it is necessary."

The officer was choked with anger. He held himself very stiffly and did not answer.

Wentworth spoke to Ram Singh in Punjabi. "I am leaving you behind, my warrior," he said. "They will undoubtedly put you in irons. In Germany, you will be put in prison. When I can, I shall come and free you."

Ram Singh's face clouded, but not, Wentworth knew, with dread of prison. It was only that he could not fight at his master's side... "Yours is the greater service, Ram Singh," Wentworth went on. "As soon as I have taken off, surrender to the captain. I'm going up and make him a prisoner now. It will be your duty to free him."

Ram Singh could not salaam, but he bowed his head. *"Han, sahib!"*

Five minutes later, Wentworth was in the cockpit of the plane; the motor was rapidly warming. He watched for Nita to put in her appearance, but she did not. After five more minutes, he waved an arm in signal, set his back against the seat, his head against the crash pad to brace for the violent jerk of the catapult's thrust. He pulled the throttle wide....

The roar almost drowned the blast of power which propelled him forward. The ship finished its short run, sagged briefly as if it were over-heavy, then soared upward into the night sky. Wentworth circled once, turned toward New York, there on the southwestern horizon, and eased the throttle to cruising speed. Twelve hundred miles from New York, five hundred from

There was a thunderous crash and the waters leaped high to engulf the enemy plane!

land… He settled himself for the long flight whose end would bring not rest, but strenuous battle….

The night hours sped swiftly. Wentworth was still above water at dawn, but a short while after, Marblehead lifted out of the sea and at eight o'clock he was only two hundred miles from New York and traveling a hundred and fifty miles an hour. He had just about enough gas to make it, he figured, though it would be safer to land and tank up….

It was a half-hour later that a ship he easily identified as the new army type of Boeing pursuit craft bulleted out of the southern sky toward him. He felt a swift rush of uneasiness. That the captain of the *Bremen* would be extremely angry, Wentworth had known, but it did not seem reasonable that the United States would go to the length of sending an army ship after him. He had expected to face arrest when he landed, but thought that his friend, Commissioner Kirkpatrick of New York, could be persuaded to kill any charges that arose….

AS THE pursuit ship raced nearer, Wentworth dug out a pair of binoculars from a pocket in the cockpit and leveled them. There were no army markers on the wings or tail. His eyes narrowed. He thrust the glasses away and yanked the throttle wide. The Boeing was not an army plane, yet it carried machine guns. The inference was obvious….

Any enemy who knew Wentworth at all well would have figured he would commandeer the catapult plane and speed back to join battle in New York. Hoffman's incomplete job was about to be finished!

The pursuit ship came on with the speed of a bullet. It was

swifter than his plane by some fifty to seventy miles an hour and there was no chance to run. Wentworth did the only thing possible, since acrobatics are impossible in a seaplane. He looked for a place to land immediately, some point where he could take cover quickly. He was above the upper end of Long Island Sound; the shores were crowded with wharves, the waters dotted with pleasure craft. If he could set the crate down swiftly, run in between two of those bulky piers, he would have protection from two sides and a chance to get ashore… He put the little seaplane into a vertical dive and held the throttle wide open.

The wind screamed through the struts and bracings. The wind tips began to vibrate and Wentworth was forced to ease up on the throttle a little. A quick backward glance showed the Boeing slanting to the attack. It was still a half-mile away, but within seconds it would come in range. Hovering to a landing on the water, Wentworth would be dead meat for the machine guns, yet if he took to the water at high speed, he might snap the pontoons off, and bring the motor down on the back of his neck. He looked thoughtfully up at the howling propeller above and behind him, peered ahead at the water.…

He saw something then which drew his lips together in a harsh line. Almost directly below him, a speed boat was bucking across the water at a pace which must top sixty miles an hour. To the south and north, two similar craft were converging. He threw back his head and laughed harshly. Whoever his enemy was, he had laid his trap thoroughly. If the Spider got out of this alive…!

Wentworth took an automatic from its clip holster and laid

it on his knees. Then his hands went back to stick and throttle. He threw another glance at the Boeing. The power dive had checked the assassin's gain for the moment... Wentworth laughed again. He dived the seaplane more steeply, headed straight for the racing boat. If they thought they could kill the Spider this easily... Now let the plane come on.

Wentworth planned to keep directly between the Boeing and the speed boat, so that any bullets that missed him would inevitably take effect on the allies of the aerial killer. When he broke from that position, he would have to contrive to be within a very short distance of the cover of those close-built piers....

He was not more than three hundred feet above the water now. He saw a man get to his feet in the speedboat, saw the flickering flame of a sub-machine gun. He ignored it. The bullets might pierce the hull of the seaplane at this distance, but they couldn't do much damage. It was the high-power weapon behind him that he feared. He threw another glance at the Boeing. It was dangerously close, within easy range. If, for one scant moment, he let the speedboat get out of the line of fire.... Apparently the men below recognized their perilous situation. They began to dodge, sending great waves washing to each side as the high-powered craft skidded on the turns.... Behind Wentworth, the Boeing darted off to the right, viraged and swept in to intercept the course of the seaplane....

IF THE pilot was skillful with his machine gun, the Spider was doomed. No matter what Wentworth did with his heavy-bottomed ship, the Boeing had only to swerve its nose a bit to pour a stream of lead into the cockpit of the seaplane....

Wentworth's lips drew apart in a grim smile. If death were coming, he would take as many of the enemy with him as possible. He spun the seaplane about and raced nose-on to meet the attack! As the Boeing swung to bring its guns to bear on him, Wentworth threw the seaplane into a dive again. For as long as he could hold those relative positions, he had his own motor partly between him and the machine gun as a shield. He had a metal propeller which would not splinter and rain deadly fragments upon him….

The Boeing's machine gun hammered, its stammering cough audible even through the beat of Wentworth's engine. The Spider, saw tracers streak past the seaplane's nose. A kick on the rudder sent him out of line, but the greedy gray smoke of the bullets followed….

Wentworth jerked his gaze from the tracer path back to the Boeing. Within moments, the attacker would have to lift its nose to avoid a collision. There would be a split-second when it passed over his head with less than twenty-five feet of clearance. That was the moment for which Wentworth had maneuvered. He caught the automatic from his lap, took the control stick from between his knees and snatched the second gun from its clip holster….

Now! The machine gun had ceased chattering. The Boeing was charging past in a three-hundred-miles-an-hour power dive. He wouldn't get in many shots, but the steady hand which had smashed clay pigeons with snap-shots should be able to hit a man at twenty-five feet, even at that terrific speed. Wentworth drew the stick of the seaplane back with his knees, slowing his own pace. Both guns blasted as quickly as he could pull the triggers… He fired first as the plane raced toward him. Then, pivoting his guns from the elbows, shifting to straight overhead, he bent backward and sent the lead streaking after the Boeing—fourteen shots bellowing out in seven jerks of the trigger fingers….

Wentworth dropped the automatics back into the cockpit, grabbed the stick just in time to tool the plane out of a stall, whipped into a headlong dive for the piers near the shore. Only then could he glance toward the Boeing. For an instant he missed it. Then there was an overwhelming crash and he saw the waters of the Sound leap high to engulf the enemy ship. It had slammed into the sea with full force, a dead hand frozen on the stick….

Behind Wentworth, the sub-machine gun in the boat was yammering, but he was rapidly outdistancing surface pursuit. The seaplane bounced noisily on the water and slowed with the drag of friction on the hull. Wentworth fed the engine, spurted for the spot between the piers which he had chosen, stopped with a heavy collision against the bulkhead and stood up to toss a line over a pile. Three men came running to the edge of the wharf. Wentworth glanced toward them and stood rigid in the cockpit, his hands shoulder high. Those three men held two revolvers and a sawed-off shotgun whose hungry black muzzle gaped at him not fifteen feet away!

"Take it, sucker!" the shotgun man shouted hoarsely. He lifted the weapon to his shoulder, sighted along its stubby barrel….

CHAPTER 3
PLAGUE CITY

WENTWORTH MADE the only possible move, though he knew in advance that it was doomed to failure. He tried to drop into the cockpit, knowing it was too small for him to wriggle into its cover quickly. A revolver shot he might dodge, but that sawed-off shotgun...! He threw himself downward, and behind him, at point-blank, deafening range, a pistol spoke!

His gaze was fixed on the man with the shotgun and he saw the head which was lowered against the stock jerk backward, saw the barrel slam upward just before the fingers closed convulsively on the triggers. The recoil of the heavy weapon gave added impetus to the man's fall, hurled him backward to the dock... And behind Wentworth, the pistol spoke twice more in a swift, calm rhythm, with a steady speed that indicated a cool head and hand. One of the two remaining gunmen drew up on tiptoes at the edge of the wharf, half-turned and pitched sideways into the water. The other threw a hurried shot at the plane and tried to flee. A bullet nailed him to the rough planking of the pier.

These things all happened while Wentworth squeezed down into the cover of the cockpit. He turned around then toward the pistol which had deafened him. The hatch of the seaplane's mail compartment was open wide enough for a gun-hand to emerge and, as he watched the cover lifted wide, he was looking into the pale, smiling face of Nita van Sloan!

27

"Now," she said weakly, "don't you wish I'd stayed on that pest ship?"

Wentworth snapped out of his amazement, for he could see that Nita was near collapse from the long hours of confinement in the tight mail compartment—from the tension of the battle when she had been helpless and those final, taut minutes when her shot had saved his life. He must hearten her, for they were not out of danger. That speed boat was racing in again, and there might be more of the killers ashore....

"Stout fellow!" he cried. "Get ashore there, and hold the fort while I collect my guns!"

He turned from her and snatched his two heavy automatics from the floor, rapidly thrust fresh clips into the butts and jacked cartridges into the chambers. He held one weapon, shoved the other into its holster, turned to give Nita a hand as she clambered from the port. She still wore that dainty garment of blue, though it was sadly crumpled now, and over it she had thrown a warm cloak. He realized what she had done, of course. The moment he had left her stateroom, she had thrown on the cloak. Even before Ram Singh had brought the officer and forced him to get the plane free, she had climbed into the mail compartment and hidden herself. He was glad, glad to have her with him and not alone for that quick shot that had saved his life a moment before. God knew that with her abroad he would have missed her steady faith, her unwavering support, in moments of stress. Yet he had not been thinking of himself when he determined to send her away....

He clambered rapidly to the deserted dock, helped Nita up

the ladder. She leaned heavily on his arm as he hurried her toward the shore. The motor roar of the speedboat, rushing in, was like the noise of a machine gun. A man in seaman's boots ran heavily into sight around the end of the dock warehouse. He checked there at sight of this man and woman in formal evening dress, each of whom gripped a gun.

"Get the police!" Wentworth shouted. "Those dope-runners tried to kill us."

The man hesitated a moment and Wentworth waved the automatic at him. "Hurry!" he shouted. "We'll hold them until you get help!"

Nita pulled her gaze from the man she had slain. "Oh, Dick," she whispered, "why did you teach me to shoot so well!"

Wentworth laughed. "Sorry that you saved my life, darling? Come on, hurry!"

They reached the end of the warehouse, started across a wide stretch of concrete pavement. Men and women were running down the streets toward the water front. Shop-keepers in white aprons stood in front of their stores, staring toward the scene of the shooting. Wentworth broke into a run. Nita was suffering the reaction of her bravery. He must keep her going until they were safe… A car rattled around a corner. The driver stepped on his brakes and stared with open mouth… Nita barely made it and Wentworth lifted her into the back of the car.

"Quickly," he barked, "get us to a hospital!"

The man only gaped. Wentworth leaned toward him. "Get us to a hospital!" he repeated sharply.

The driver whipped about, and the car wheezed away. He was almost beyond the limits of the town before he turned his head around again. "Say," he said, "they ain't no hospital nearer'n Stamford...."

Wentworth bargained swiftly with the man, bought the wreck of a car at an outrageous price and took over the driving. He left the previous owner grinning after him. Nita was sitting up weakly again. She smiled faintly. "Silly of me," she whispered. "I don't usually act the old-fashioned girl."

Wentworth smiled warmly upon her, "When we get to a place where we can stop for a few moments," he told her, "I'm going to rail at you for coming... and then I'm going to tell you what a wonderful creature you are!"

Nita laughed, her strength rapidly returning. "Oh, Mithter Wentworth," she lisped, "can't you thtop now?"

STATE POLICE stopped them well outside the New York City line. There was a quarantine; no one could enter or leave the city. Wentworth could have explained that they were already exposed to the dread disease, but it would have involved delay. The men were staring curiously at them anyway—a man and a woman in exquisite evening dress, driving a dilapidated car whose engine, even idling, made so much noise it was difficult to hear. Wentworth's card from Commissioner Kirkpatrick got them past finally. Even before they went to Wentworth's home, they stopped at a hospital and had themselves treated with cholera inoculations....

"It is useless if we're already infected," Wentworth told Nita, "but I'm beginning to hope that we escaped on the ship." He smiled. "We confined our drinking there pretty much to wine, and we'd better continue to do so!"

They rattled along a strangely empty Fifth Avenue. The double-deck buses were almost without passengers and the rich department stores had a barren appearance. The deep-throated wails of ambulance sirens made a melancholy background for the close heat of the day.

Those people remaining upon the streets seemed weighed down by an overwhelming grief. Even the ragamuffins who usually romped in the park were gone. God help a city when the very children forget to play!

Three people waited on a corner for a bus: a girl, a man, an older woman. They huddled together there and now and again they glanced about them anxiously. The girl gripped the woman's arm and suddenly the older woman sprang away, stiffening with the scream that tore through her body. She was bending forward slowly, agonizingly over the clutching hands with which she dug at her body. She pitched sideways to the pavement, writhed there, crying out hoarsely. The man who had been with them turned and ran, heedless, panicked, along the hot pavements.

Wentworth jerked the car to a halt. "Nita, get a taxi and go to the apartment," he said quietly. "I'll take this woman to a hospital."

A slight, wan smile touched Nita's lips. "I'll drive," she stated. "You help the girl with her."

All the way to the hospital, the girl kept up a faint moaning as she supported the older woman, evidently her mother. She rocked back and forth to the rhythm of her slow pain, scarcely seemed conscious of what was happening. As Wentworth helped carry the mother into the hospital, the daughter screamed and fell in convulsions on the floor.

Wentworth noticed that both women were carried to beds which stood in the choked hospital halls and his lips thinned as he realized how crowded conditions must be. An interne glanced at them curiously and Wentworth abruptly remembered their dress. He led Nita heavily back to the car....

Wentworth's butler, Jenkyns, had closed the penthouse on Fifth Avenue, except for the servant's quarters which he shared with the chauffeur, Jackson. Yet, with only an hour's warning, he had the place in entire readiness. When he had bowed them in, he hurried away to prepare lunch. Jenkyns had never been able to find a *chef* who, he thought, could adequately serve his master, and Wentworth was as well pleased to keep his household to the absolute minimum. These three who served him, Jackson, Jenkyns and Ram Singh, he could safely trust with his secrets and his life. He had done so many times....

WENTWORTH ESCORTED Nita to the suite she always occupied in times of stress—it had a complete wardrobe—and stopped to telephone Commissioner Kirkpatrick before he changed his own clothing. His call was put through to headquarters without question....

"I've been expecting you to call," Kirkpatrick told him, in his clipped accents. "I have a complaint from the captain of the

Bremen asking me to arrest you for the theft of the ship's plane. They have Ram Singh in chains."

Wentworth told him briefly what had happened and of the airplane attack. Kirkpatrick exclaimed sharply: "But, Dick, who under the sun…?" His words cut off and he went on slowly. "There has been a rather curious murder. I have had no detailed report on it because the alarm came only about an hour ago. It seems that Christian Daly has been murdered, and the killer took time afterward to draw a mysterious design in ink on his chest."

Wentworth frowned into the transmitter. Apparently, Kirkpatrick saw no connection between the cholera outbreak and the attack aboard the ship. He had made no mention of the epidemic in the city, but of course the police would have very little to do with that unless Wentworth's own suspicions were confirmed….

The murder was curious. Christian Daly was a banker with wide investments.

"What sort of design was this on Daly's chest?" Wentworth queried somberly.

Kirkpatrick laughed shortly. "That's the ridiculous part of it. The murderer played a game of tic-tac-toe on Daly's chest!"

Wentworth said, "What?" His voice was incredulous. It was ridiculous, that childish game! A design of two vertical lines, and two horizontal lines cutting through them at right-angles, forming a design of nine rectangles, only one of which was completely enclosed. Two opponents then used marks, usually an X opposed to a circle, and each taking alternate turns, tried

NITA VAN SLOAN

to place three of his symbols in a straight line before the oppo-
nent could interpose his own mark. It didn't make sense that a
murderer....

"Do you suppose it has some meaning?" he asked Kirkpatrick,
"or is it just a trick to confuse the police?"

Kirkpatrick replied slowly that he did not know, said that he had been on the point of going to Daly's home.

"If you don't mind," Wentworth told him, "I'll join you there as soon as I can change my clothing... By the way Kirk, have you found the source of contamination in this cholera epidemic?"

"The entire city water supply," Kirkpatrick told him briefly. "They can't discover where, originally, the germs came from."

WENTWORTH HUNG up, stood staring with eyes that saw nothing at the book-lined wall of his study, from which he was talking. The entire city water supply was infected with cholera! Last night, there had been seventy-five seizures. Heaven alone knew how many had been stricken since then. If the entire city water supply contained the germs, this day and the next would see literally thousands laid low with cholera... Wentworth rasped a curse, swung, striding, toward his personal suite. He could not criticize Kirkpatrick's failure to suspect human agency in the epidemic, but there could be no other reasonable explanation. It was incredible that the entire water supply of New York's millions coming from a half-dozen sources, should become simultaneously infected with cholera when, never before

in the city's history, had such a thing happened. There had been a cholera epidemic in New York, certainly, but it had had its origin in plague cases from ships....

Wentworth was rapidly changing from his evening dress. A brief shower and he was pulling on the dark tweeds that he always preferred. He swiftly strapped on the shoulder holster for his two heavy automatics. He strode from his suite, met Jenkyns in the hallway....

"Master Dick!" the aged man servant cried, "I've prepared lunch...!"

Wentworth checked, smiling at him. "My hat and sword-cane, Jenkyns. Tell Miss Nita...."

He saw Nita herself down the hall and hurried toward her. "Kirkpatrick told me of a strange murder, dear," he said, "Christian Daly."

She took his hands, her eyes widening. "Oh, poor Evelyn," she cried softly. "Wait a minute, Dick, and I'll go with you."

"His daughter, this Evelyn?" Wentworth asked.

Nita was hurrying away down the hall. "His ward, I think," she called back. "There was some mystery about it...."

She came back within a few minutes, a close, turban-like hat poised jauntily on her chestnut curls. Her suit was dark silk, and Wentworth noticed that the handbag she carried was large enough to hold the automatic he had given her.

A taxi sped them northward along Fifth Avenue's empty length. Even the absence of people was an ominous thing. Wentworth's lips were tautened into a stiff, unsmiling line.

"I have a feeling we should have waited to eat," he said quietly. "It may be quite a while...."

NITA LAID a gloved hand comically against her stomach. "I have that feeling, too," she said. Wentworth laughed in spite of himself. Well he understood that Nita, as always was trying to keep his spirits up when the battle was on... His cheerfulness was short-lived. The empty streets were a challenge. Fear already had the people by the throats. God alone knew where this tragedy would end....

The taxi cut sharply to the right, entered high iron gates into a short, semicircular drive cut out of the side of a building. Wentworth recognized Daly's home. There was a morgue wagon, and Kirkpatrick's bullet-proof sedan steady there. Other police cars lined the curb... A policeman at the door raised his club in respectful salute as Wentworth bowed Nita in.

"Upstairs, sir," he said, "in the room to the right. The Commissioner expects you."

Nita took her hand from Wentworth's arm. "You go ahead," she requested. "I'll find Evelyn and be around somewhere."

Wentworth nodded and took the stairs in double-step strides, turned into the room which the policeman had indicated and stopped abruptly, staring with narrow eyes. Christian Daly had been stabbed through the base of the throat as he sat upright in a high-backed chair by the window of his study. It was apparent that the knife's point, protruding at the back and piercing the wood of the chair, held his body upright. Bathed in the warm sunlight spreading through the window, he was a pitiful spectacle. Commissioner Kirkpatrick had evidently just arrived.

He stood staring, grim-faced at the body. He looked up, nodded to Wentworth with a grim twist of his straight lips.

"It's not pretty," he said. "No prints on the hilt of the knife. No one was upstairs here with him at all except his ward, Evelyn. He was seen to come upstairs at noon. At one o'clock, a servant came to tell him lunch was ready and found him like this!"

Wentworth's thoughts were racing swiftly, beyond this murder, to the epidemic that had sunk its fangs in to the city, to the overwhelming attacks upon himself. What in the name of heaven was behind all this? What was the reason for the slaughter?

He said quietly, "The window was open?"

Kirkpatrick shrugged, "The knife might have been shot from

outside, but how about those symbols on his chest, that ridiculous business of tic-tac-toe?"

Wentworth crossed to the body, bent over to inspect the blue tracery on the dead flesh. Christian Daly's shirt had been ripped open after the knife had killed him—there was blood on both the outside and inside of the garment—and these figures scrawled on his chest in blue ink. There were five of the diagrams, each one representing a game of tic-tac-toe and in the final one, there were three circles in a row, with a straight line drawn through them, signifying a victory for the user of that symbol. Wentworth straightened, shook his head.

"You're photographing that, of course."

Kirkpatrick nodded, "Of course."

"I'd like a copy, if you don't mind," Wentworth said. "I've an idea that there's a message hidden in that. If you'll notice, all of the signs are not identical. Meantime, I'll make a copy of them…" He drew out a pencil and paper and, as nearly as possible, made an exact copy of the four diagrams upon the chest of the dead man, stood looking down at them….

Kirkpatrick frowned. "If that's a code message of some kind, it's a very clever one. That victory indicated on the last diagram, the one with a line drawn through three circles in a row, might mean that the killer was wiping out an old score…."

"It might," Wentworth agreed, "but I doubt it. There's more to this…."

The scream was shrill and frightened, a woman crying out in terror and, before its echoes had died, Wentworth had whirled and was racing down the wide steps. He darted into the drawing room, found Nita holding a girl close in her arms. The window was broken and, in the opposite wall, a knife had buried a third of its blade.

"Some one threw a knife through the window," Nita called clearly. "It didn't miss Evelyn by six inches."

Wentworth darted to the window, stared out into the street, but there was no one in sight, no car except those of the police, jammed close together at the curb. He turned as Kirkpatrick stormed into the room.

"It appears," Wentworth said quietly, "that some one is intent on wiping out the Daly family."

CHAPTER 4
BATTLE FOR A CITY

AS IF Wentworth's pronouncement had been a signal, a disturbance broke out at the entrance to the Daly home. A policeman's voice lifted hoarsely in a gruff order and another man replied sharply, angrily. Kirkpatrick snapped another command and a uniformed officer went out hastily, returned a few moments later thrusting a man before him.

The man moved stubbornly, resisting the officer's hand on his shoulder. His head was bare and a heavy lock of brown hair fell lankly across his forehead. His cheeks were flushed.

"What does all this mean?" he demanded excitedly. "First the police won't let me in, and then… Evelyn, darling, what's the matter?"

Evelyn Daly pulled away from Nita and ran to the man,

threw her arms about him and began to sob against his chest. The policeman spoke in a whisper that might as well have been a shout: "This here is Carnes, Daly's secretary, Mr. Commissioner," he blatted. "You remember the butler says they had a big row this morning?"

Kirkpatrick nodded, his eyes fixed on Bill Carnes as the secretary looked defiantly toward him over Evelyn's shaking shoulder: "What's this all about?" he demanded again bitterly.

Kirkpatrick stepped quietly forward, "Can you throw a knife, Carnes?" he asked.

Carnes said, "What the hell…?" Then he glimpsed the knife sticking in the wall, and his face paled, his arms tightened about the girl. "I can throw knives, yes, but I certainly didn't throw that one!"

Kirkpatrick went on softly. "But you did *kill* Christian Daly a while ago, eh, Carnes?"

Evelyn whipped up her glossy black head, whirled toward Kirkpatrick. "Oh, why do you behave this way? Of course Bill didn't do it! Anybody would know that. Just because father didn't want us to marry yet…."

Carnes gasped, "Good God, is Mr. Daly dead?"

Wentworth watched with intent, steady eyes. He liked the boy's spirit. Evelyn… He turned his attention to her, studied the fine, long lines of her face. Despite the sudden warping of grief, it was patrician. She had her shoulder against Bill's chest, his arm about her, more as protection to him than to herself.

"Why must police be so stupid?" she cried. "Do you think Bill would have tried to kill me with that knife?" She aimed

41

a pointing forefinger toward the weapon in the wall.

Kirkpatrick shook his head. "But he might have thrown it as a blind, because we would know he wouldn't throw it at you. I'm afraid we'll have to take you in for further investigation, Carnes."

"But it's stupid!" Evelyn Daly cried.

Wentworth smiled slightly, moved toward Nita. If he read the signs right, Kirkpatrick wasn't going to take Bill Carnes to jail quite yet. There was a certain tension in the way Carnes stood, headstrong defiance in the lift of his clean jaw....

"I'm not guilty, sir," Carnes insisted. "I swear I didn't even know that Mr. Daly was dead until you told me a moment ago. I swear it, sir." He hesitated, looking from one of his accusers to another. "What time was he killed, anyway?"

The Commissioner eyed him steadily. "About half-past twelve, the medical examiner believes... Why?"

Carnes was frowning, worried. "I don't want to accuse anyone falsely, sir, but since you're accusing me... Has his appointment book been examined?"

Kirkpatrick shook his head. "No appointment book was found in his office. I looked for it especially."

Carnes cried out in triumph. "But he has one, sir! And he had an appointment at a quarter past twelve today!"

42

Wentworth thrust forward asked, "With whom, Carnes?"

"With Mr. Ralds, of the Amity Trust Company, sir." Carnes turned back eagerly to Kirkpatrick. "I'm not accusing Mr. Ralds, sir. But you see, other people have been here to see Mr. Daly!"

KIRKPATRICK SMILED slightly. "A good try, Carnes, but the butler denies admitting anyone after twelve o'clock. Of course, it's barely possible that Daly came downstairs and let Ralds in himself...."

Wentworth understood that Kirkpatrick was trying to infuriate Carnes into incriminating himself. He doubted that the Commissioner really suspected the secretary....

"Surely, Kirk," Wentworth put in quietly. "You don't think Carnes concocted those cryptic symbols?"

"That could be a blind. I'm sorry, Carnes," Kirkpatrick said, "but you'll have to go with us."

Carnes tightened his arm about Evelyn Daly. Then he thrust her aside briskly, reached the broken window in two long strides and tumbled through it. A police man cursed, but it was Wentworth who acted first. He sprang across the room to the window, automatic leaping into his hand from its underarm holster. He lifted it carefully as Bill Carnes sprinted for the cover of the corner that was diagonally opposite. Wentworth aimed the gun very slowly. The policeman behind him laughed. "Don't need to hurry. When Mr. Wentworth shoots them, they stay shot."

Carnes was almost at the corner, Wentworth squeezed the trigger and Carnes kept on running, rounded into the cross-street out of sight. Wentworth turned about, his face strange with surprise.

"Can you imagine that?" he exclaimed. "I missed him!"

Nita lifted a quick hand to her smiling lips. Kirkpatrick's blue eyes held a frosty glitter; his lips beneath the black pointed mustache were thin with anger.

"You're going to overplay your hand one of these times, Dick," he said harshly. "If I could prove you didn't try…!" He broke off, whirled as Evelyn darted at Wentworth, her clenched fists beating at him.

"You tried to kill Bill!" she gasped. "You tried to kill him…!" Her tiny fists drummed against his chest.

Wentworth threw his arms about Evelyn, held her while fury reddened her face, while her black hair rippled loose and fell in waves upon her shoulders. *You tried to kill Bill!*

"If you would listen to Mr. Kirkpatrick," Wentworth suggested, "you would learn that he doubts that very much. He thinks I prevented the police from catching Bill just because they were so sure I'd hit him that they didn't even try. Police are almost superstitious about my accuracy with an automatic, Miss Daly."

The girl's furious strength was expended. She collapsed against Wentworth, no longer fighting, but sobbing brokenly, her whole body convulsed with grief. Wentworth had to hold her now to keep her from falling. Nita came rapidly forward, her violet eyes very gentle as she put her arms about Evelyn.

"You mustn't blame her, Dick," she said softly. "She's very much upset." She led Evelyn out of the room.…

A policeman came panting in. "He got clean away, sir. We were so sure Mr. Wentworth would hit him… Geez! I hadn't oughta run like that! I…!" His mouth stayed open, and an expression of pained surprise flashed over his face. He doubled over slowly and pitched to the floor, writhing.

Kirkpatrick cursed, "Get this man to a hospital quickly! It's the cholera…!" Color drained from his lean, healthy face. "That makes ten thousand and seventy cases," he added thickly.

"Ten thousand!" Wentworth cried. "Good God! I knew it was inevitable, but this quickly…! Kirk, don't you realize there must be a human agency directing this epidemic?"

"Human agency?" Kirkpatrick stared at him, eyes narrowing. "You mean that some criminal has loosed cholera on the city for his own ends? But damn it, Dick, even a criminal…."

He stopped, biting his lips, and Wentworth smiled slightly, knowing he was recalling other occasions when criminals had vented their megalomaniac fury in wholesale slaughter. "Damn it, Dick, there's no *reason* in it! Have you any proof?"

WENTWORTH LAUGHED shortly. "Proof? I have all the proof I need. Never before has there been a cholera epidemic in New York from contamination of water supply. And the city's sanitary condition is better than at any previous time in its history. How could cholera abruptly gather so much headway now…? Furthermore, do you believe it would be possible for ten thousand people to be stricken overnight from a mere contami-

nation of the water supply? Ridiculous! No, Kirkpatrick, someone has infected the city's whole water-shed with cholera…."

"And you let that boy get away!"

Wentworth arched his brows slightly as Kirkpatrick bellowed
the accusation. So Kirkpatrick also figured that there was some
connection between the cholera and the tic-tac-toe murders?

"Really, Kirk," he drawled, "the man was not my prisoner. I
merely did my best to stop him for you. So far as that's concerned,
I could wager that, if he is guilty—which I doubt—he will be
of more use to you free than a prisoner. You have only to keep
watch over Miss Daly, with a view to forming contact with Bill
Carnes…" His lips twisted. "It's a rather ancient trick, getting a
man through his woman."

Kirkpatrick's anger evaporated as quickly as it had risen. He
looked at Wentworth curiously, but made no reply. Wentworth
shrugged. "I suppose you'll check on Sam Ralds, though I don't
see what motive he could possibly have for killing Daly."

"No," Kirkpatrick said, his eyes still on Wentworth's. "But
we'll check, of course. Dick, that offer I made of making you
my deputy is still open. I could use you beautifully, and it would
give you authority you don't have now. I wouldn't interfere with
your work too much!"

Wentworth shrugged impatiently. Kirkpatrick's interfer-
ence—that job of deputy commissioner—would rob him of the
one thing that made him powerful: the fact that he punished
criminals swiftly and certainly, without regard to the due
processes of law. They had been over that same ground so often.
They were closest friends, he and Kirkpatrick, and the identity of

One plane was plunging earthward with a comet's tail of fire behind it!

the Spider was an unacknowledged fact between them. Yet the Commissioner was not a man to shirk his duty. He had warned Wentworth: "If evidence of your being the Spider ever comes into my hands, Dick, I'll prosecute you to the limit of my power." It remained like that between them, and Wentworth made sure that the evidence should not fall into Kirkpatrick's hands… Nita came into the room quietly and Wentworth's eyes went to hers.

"I gave Evelyn a sleeping powder," she said softly. "I think she'll be all right now."

WENTWORTH SUCKED in a deep breath, shrugged aside the depression that gripped him. "What's being done to purify the water system, Kirk?" he asked shortly. "The authorities are undoubtedly aware that the best bet is to use hydrochloric acid. A solution of one half of one percent will kill cholera germs in six minutes. If there's pepsin present, an even weaker solution will work."

Kirkpatrick nodded, his eyes keenly on Wentworth. "There are three train loads of hydrochloric acid on the way to the city now. There wasn't enough on hand here to do any good. The trains should arrive sometime tonight."

"How strong a guard has been put on them?" Wentworth asked.

Kirkpatrick shook his head. "None."

Wentworth took a short half-step forward. "Good lord, Kirk, that's fatal! There should be a full company of militia with each train. You can have them met at the state line… Even if you don't believe some criminal is behind this disaster, the precaution will do no harm. Listen, you get hold of the governor. I'm going to get my plane and fly to meet those trains…."

Kirkpatrick nodded slowly. Wentworth whirled to Nita. "You keep an eye on Evelyn, dear, and I'll see you…."

Nita shook her head, smiling, her eyes very steady. "Dick, I told you that wherever you go, I'm going, too. I thought we'd settled that once and for all."

For a moment, Wentworth hesitated, then he clasped her shoulders. There was a warmth within him. Damn it, he *needed* Nita with him. He felt a rise of spirits, he was laughing when he faced Kirkpatrick again.

"They don't stand a chance!" he cried. "Nita's going with me."

Kirkpatrick bowed with the grave formality that was his. "I would be glad of such an ally," he agreed quietly.

All Wentworth's depression went from him. He was abruptly gay. His hand clasped Nita's as they left the room. They might have been walking by a brook in spring, instead of going forth to battle again callous murderers. The mood continued as they rode behind Jackson to the flying field and climbed into Wentworth's speedy, scarlet Northrup with machine guns mounted in the forward cockpit. Wentworth turned about and smiled at Nita, who was tucking her silken curls under a close-fitting summer helmet….

The air was heavy and dead with heat as the Northrup raced, like a scarlet flame, across the field. It was a perfect day for flying, but there would be local thunder showers to dodge. Wentworth hummed inaudibly—even to himself—as the ship split the air. Three quarters of an hour and they would be hovering over the first of the acid trains, filled with tiers of glass carboys piled row on row in box cars—highly concentrated acid which would corrode anything other than glass. By now national guardsmen and state police were converging on the tracks in motor trucks. They would mount guard along the right of way, ride the trains. But they were late, late... These things should have been done long ago. How would the men of the enemy strike? That they had armed planes Wentworth knew. Bombs from the sky? It was possible, but not necessary. A machine gun stationed beside the right of way to smash the carboys would accomplish just as much, and far more terribly....

IT WAS a little less than three quarters of an hour later when Wentworth spotted a long freight train racing along the track. He swung in wide circles high above it, watching. The sky held no suspicion of another plane. He felt a mounting tension. That train would mean salvation to countless persons in New York, where ten thousand had been stricken in a single day. Damn it, the train *should* race at top speed....

There, five miles ahead, was the place where the guardsmen were to board it. The heavy trucks stood at the station, the men standing about them, waiting. Wentworth shot ahead of the train, circled over the station, scanned the woods that crowded close to the tracks on either side. They were in full leaf now, and it was difficult to see the ground. *What was that?*

Wentworth glimpsed a gleam as of metal there in the edge of the trees nearest the station. He swung swiftly about to peer downward more carefully. There it was again! Damn it, was it possible that the criminals spreading this fiendish plague had learned of the plans for guarding the train and were ready to strike at the very moment when…?

"Take the controls!" Wentworth shouted to Nita, forgetting the phones which connected them. Then he lowered his voice, spoke swiftly: "In the edge of the woods, I think I see a machine gun emplacement. But I can't be sure. I'm going overside in a parachute. If I'm wrong, nothing's lost. You can pick me up in that field a half mile to the west of the tracks. If I'm right…."

"I'll drop a warning to the soldiers," Nita added. "All right, I've got the controls." There wasn't a tremor in her voice, though she knew that Wentworth was planning single-handed to attack a machine-gun nest. Wentworth thanked her silently for that quiet courage as he stepped across the wing and dived headfirst toward the ground. The earth spun dizzily until he jerked the rip-cord and the parachute snapped him upright. He could see the train, barely a mile down the track, could hear its whistle blaring hoarsely. He peered toward the station, saw soldiers form a swift, ragged line and aim their rifles upward. The fools! Didn't they know—hadn't they been told—that he was here to help them?

Before they began to fire, the scarlet Northrup ripped down past him, interposing its bulk as a shield between him and the rifle men below. Nita spun in a tight circle there, drawing closer and closer to the ground. He saw her message plunge to the soldiers overside in a tiny parachute. The spiteful crack of the rifles reached him thinly. Men scattered from the drifting message. Fools! Did they think bombs were dropped on parachutes?

51

Wentworth was within three hundred feet of the ground now and the thick tops of the trees seemed to be clustering beneath his feet. He could no longer see that furtive gleam of metal, but it must be there, almost directly under him. There was a jumble of rocks on the edge of the right of way, a perfect emplacement for a machine gun. If he were to land in a clear spot—he could guide the parachute to an extent by pulling on the shrouds, by spilling air from under the 'chute on the side opposite the direction in which he wished to move—it would have to be directly in front of that pile of rocks—in front of the muzzle of the machine gun he was increasingly sure was hidden there! His only alternative was to land in a tree-top. His lips tightened, and he selected the wide crest of a maple almost exactly over the spot where he had caught sight of what seemed to be a gun. He tugged on the shrouds, threw another swift glance toward Nita and the plane. He was aware that the rifles had ceased to speak. Nita was swooping low over the station. The thunder of the locomotive was heavy and deep. Within a space of seconds, it would be slowing for the stop—to load the soldiers....

THE TREE-TOP reached leafy arms for Wentworth and his legs crashed into the thin, topmost branches. Something jabbed his left calf like a knife; then he slammed solidly across a limb, jarred to his very brain by the impact. Already his hands were working, not at the shrouds, but at ripping his automatics from their sheaths while his eyes quested the ground below. He saw a man dart out of cover with a Thompson gun in his hands, staring up toward where he was perched. Instantly, the muzzle lifted, sprayed lead through the limbs. Wentworth sent his Spider laughter downward, lifted the right hand automatic and fired once. The machine gunner was nailed to the earth. His heels flew high and he rolled until he hit against a tree trunk. The gun rooted its muzzle into the ground, like a hog.

Cautiously, Wentworth thrust one automatic back into its holster, worked on the buckles of the harness. Moments later, he was dropping stealthily from limb to limb, eyes glued on the spot from which that killer had emerged. No one else had shown himself, but other men might be lying in wait, well concealed…. The thunder of the train was very near Wentworth now, and through its deep roar, he caught the staccato hammer of a machine gun. No short bursts these, but continuous fire. The train, which should have clapped on its brakes for the station, pounded straight ahead with roaring exhausts, and Wentworth had a glimpse of the engineer, sprawled bloodily on the floor of his cab.

With an oath, Wentworth swung wide on a limb, let it bow far down with him, and dropped full twenty feet to the earth. He landed lightly on his toes, knees bent, spun in a tumbler's somersault on his shoulders and came up behind a tree. An automatic blasted viciously at him from somewhere in that pile of rocks and the machine gun's cackle continued….

There was an acrid odor in the air, the smell of deadly chlorine gas. The acid…! Wentworth flung himself wide of the tree behind which he had taken cover, saw the gunman who was blasting at him. His own two guns barked a single note and the man was hurled violently backward under the double impact of lead. With a harsh shout, Wentworth charged!

Beyond the rocks, he could see the fleeting sides of the boxcars, the seam of bullet-holes sewn across their flimsy wood. Liquid streamed from their bottoms, lifting first a white smoke like steam, then swirling clouds of yellowish green—chlorine! The acid, and the steel trucks and rails, were combining to throw off that deadly gas!

Wentworth leaped to the top of a rock, glimpsed a man with white face twist about with a powerful, tripod machine gun. He saw the weapon whipped about to bear on him, but it was heavy and awkward… There was a grim smile on the Spider's lips as he lifted an automatic. Because of this man and his machine gun, a trainload of acid which might have saved thousands of lives in New York City would never reach its goal; because of him, the rails, eaten away with acid, would not bear the following trains. This man was a multiple murderer, a wanton assassin… Wentworth's automatic beaded on the man's head and he squeezed the trigger. One shot was enough.

Wentworth sprang forward to the machine gun, seeking more of the enemy. He peered up at the train. The riddled box cars were streaming acid from every crack and from beneath the trucks, the yellowish green fumes of chlorine rose like a poisonous steam where the acid met the steel. Even as he watched, a box car jumped from the acid-corroded tracks, and dragging a half-dozen others after it, went ploughing and crashing from the right of way. With caught breath, Wentworth watched the runaway. For a hundred feet it went on its tottering course, upright though swaying. Two hundred, three… Swerving like an infuriated bull, it headed straight for the station and the close-grouped, paralyzed soldiers!

IT WAS as if that juggernaut of fury were actually imbued with the same hatred which filled the Master of the Plague—the demon who had caused this thing! The foremost car struck a motor lorry and sent it spinning like a toy. Men in uniform were running now, their faces white. Their screams were drowned in the all-enveloping roar of the runaway train. The leading car struck the station with an unbelievable impact, ploughed through. The roof of the station tilted crazily, jaunty as a debutante's hat, then collapsed. Two of the following cars pyramided, pawing the air with their spinning wheels like rearing gargantuan horses. The tail of the train whip-lashed around and burst asunder. A tidal wave of death-acid washed the national guardsmen from the face of the earth…!

Wentworth was pale to the lips as he watched; great, ragged curses tore from his throat. The thick-clustered soldiers had no chance to escape. The hungry acid seized upon them, lapping playfully about their feet. Men's legs were stripped bare of flesh in an instant; hamstrung, they tumbled into the devouring liquid. Others, splashed by the hell-fluid, tried to flee and were robbed of strength as it ate into their vitals. They screamed piteously until the end….

Where, a few moments before, a hundred and fifty men had clustered, a bare twenty had escaped. The victims lay in sodden, vanishing heaps which disintegrated under the assault of the concentrated add. Wentworth realized that the Plague Master had planned this deliberately. In some way, he had learned where the troopers would board the train and he had set up his machine gun nest, intending that the spraying acid should slaughter the helpless soldiers!

The air was full of the acrid rasp of chlorine. Wentworth strangled, pressed a handkerchief to his nostrils and mouth and fled along the woods path. He had slain the wrecker crew, but what had that accomplished? More than a hundred men lay dead—horribly murdered—along the right of way. The mercy load which might have saved New York's thousands lay wasted there, destroying tracks, withering the very grass and trees. Good God, he must warn those other two trains that followed! They could not travel on these acid-eaten rails. They must go some other way. Heaven grant that they had not already fallen prey to the savage butchers....

Wentworth blundered out onto a road threw up his hands in the path of a car which was roaring ahead with a wide-open engine. The car bucked, skidded on the brakes, rocked along an uneven shoulder and came to a halt fifty feet beyond him with its nose against a small tree. The car immediately backed up and a man spilled out of the driver's seat, dragging a shotgun behind him.

"What the hell happened up here?" he demanded.

"Wreck," Wentworth shouted, running toward him. "Spilled acid all over the station. There must be a hundred dead... Quickly, where can I reach a telephone?"

The man whirled back to the car and lurched it in a tight circle back the way he had come as Wentworth sprang to the running board.

"I heard shooting!" he shouted. The car was already in high, leaping forward with increasing speed. "You better get inside. The road curves…" Wentworth clambered into the back seat. He swiftly related what had happened, for he had recognized authority in this man. He was an official of some sort. He could hear the man rasping curses. His hands were clamped tight on the steering wheel and he took the curves heeling far over, tires shrieking. He dodged past a truck on a bend, just barely dodged a heavy sedan speeding in the opposite direction. After that, he kicked the siren whenever he neared curves….

"We'll go straight into Harmonville!" he shouted over his shoulder. "There are phones along here, but we wouldn't save much time."

WENTWORTH LEANED over the door and peered back at the sky. The Northrup was no longer in sight. Nita must have set it down in that field he had indicated before bailing out. He hoped that she wouldn't go to the station. That chlorine wasn't strong, but it might be strong enough….

A town opened up ahead and the siren blasted wide open. Autos skittered out of the road. The driver hurtled the curb into a small parkway, raced to the steps of the courthouse and raced inside, Wentworth just behind him. He flung a hand at an office.

"Get a phone in there. You take care of the other trains, I'll get the hospital…."

Wentworth slammed into the office, snatched a phone off a man's desk. The man flinched back, sat with his hands braced on the chair arms, his eyes wide.

"The Governor of the State," Wentworth snapped at the

operator. "He's probably in his office at the State Building. Richard Wentworth calling. This number…? Forget it, this is life and death business!"

He looked over the instrument at the startled man, smiled slightly. "There's been a train wreck down the road three or four miles," he said. "Sorry to burst in on you like this…."

The man answered limply: "That's… that's quite all right!"

Wentworth finished his phoning, went into the hall again, looking for the man who had driven him to town. The other two trains were to be stopped a dozen miles up the line and held on a siding for an adequate escort of troops. They'd get planes there, too.

The reaction had set in now and Wentworth was beginning to feel a little fatigued. He realized that he had been flying the entire night before, that it was getting near dinner time and he had eaten only hurriedly with Nita while they were at the airport. This was out of his hands now. He had proved his point to Kirkpatrick. There could no longer be any doubt that there was human agency behind the cholera. He thought it might be a good plan to go back to those men he had killed and see if there was any kind of identification upon them. Men of their criminal class usually worked in certain, fixed groups. If you could identify one member, you had a pretty good idea of those working with him.

Wentworth strode out the front door. The car which had brought him was gone. He heard the beat of a plane's motor and glanced up. The Northrup, *Nita*… She was flying northward across the town at low altitude, motor roaring wide-open. He could tell that by the heavy throb....

A chill touched Wentworth's spine. Nita was flying into battle, into danger. He could not doubt it. For no other reason would she have discarded their plans....

Wentworth hit the pavement running. There was an old car parked at the curb with a card in its windshield that read: *Taxi*. The driver was asleep. Wentworth shook him violently. "Quick," he barked. "Follow that plane!"

The man blinked. "Listen, mister, this here ain't no airyplane. I can't...."

Wentworth said harshly: "Get moving!" His voice was like a whip lash.

The man gagged, "Yes, sir," his face startled, and kicked the starter. The motor sounded sweet, Wentworth observed with relief. He hung on the running board, watching the Northrup fading into the northern sky. "Is there an airport near here?" he demanded. "A place where I can rent a ship?"

THE CAR was bellowing along the main street, its motor throaty and deep. "Can't rightly call it no airport," the driver stated slowly, "but there's a fellow out here takes people up riding and things on Sundays."

"Take me there!" Wentworth snapped. He offered money for speed and got it, up to a certain point. The car couldn't top seventy.

It took fifteen minutes to reach the field. The plane was standing there with a cold motor, a low-winged monoplane job which looked capable of doing a hundred and twenty miles an hour in a pinch. Wentworth groaned. It was better than the car, of course, but slow, slow....

He paid the driver and ran toward the small, sheet-iron shack which served as an office. A man in dungarees came to the door, staring curiously.

"Get your motor going," Wentworth shouted at him. "Quick!"

The man hesitated. The driver of the taxi got slowly to the ground and leaned against the door, staring. Wentworth understood the flier's hesitancy. Too many criminals had used planes for a getaway, and his hurry was suspicious... Wentworth explained his needs in quick, staccato sentences, showed the police-card he carried from New York headquarters. The flier snatched up a helmet....

"No," Wentworth countermanded sharply. "I want the plane myself. There may be fighting and I can't risk your life. If the plane is damaged..." He snatched out a check book, hastily wrote a check and handed it to the man. "There's some insurance. Now, get that plane going!"

The man was still frowning as he kicked the motor over, set it at warming speed and climbed down again beside Wentworth. "Be careful, sir," he pleaded, "that plane's my whole stake."

Wentworth climbed into the cockpit, found a helmet and strapped it tight under his chin. He watched the engine-heat indicator impatiently. He peered again and again into the north, where Nita had long since vanished in the Northrup. Finally, the motor was warm enough and he signaled contact, whirled into the wind and shot the plane into the sky. The plane surprised him, climbing with remarkable speed and tossing off a better pace than he had anticipated, nearly one-eighty....

Wentworth kept his eyes trained on the northern sky, glancing now and again at the railway tracks which slanted off a little to the Northeast. A dozen miles from here was the junction where the trains were to wait before being turned onto another route for New York....

He tensed abruptly in his seat. Those whirling specks there to northward! Was he mad, or were those planes spinning and dodging in a dogfight? Three of them, and one would be Nita in the Scarlet Northrup. Good God above! Nita was an excellent pilot, but that sort of thing called for acrobatics of the highest type. Thank Heaven that at least she had machine guns....

A cry that was a prayer squeezed through Wentworth's clenched teeth. One of the planes was plunging downward with a comet's tail of fire behind it, plunging in a devil's spin of destruction, wrapped in searing gasoline flame, while the two other ships performed acrobatics of joy above. It couldn't be Nita. *It couldn't be....!* Wentworth did not consider the fact that he was hurling himself into a battle against planes equipped with machine guns whereas he carried only his two automatics. He thought only of Nita, gone bravely to fight his battles and now, perhaps, dying in the flames....

CHAPTER 5
DISASTER!

WENTWORTH DID not know when he yanked the throttle wide on the plane, but he became aware presently of the trembling vibration that the engine sent through the ship. Something was off-balance somewhere. If it continued, it might shake the plane to pieces. But he could not lessen the mad pace; there was death in the northern sky. It might be that Nita had plunged down in flames... He held the throttle open, tried to ignore the quaking of the ship. If only one of those planes still circling, dodging across the sky was the Northrup! Hope was beginning to swell within him. If both of those planes were enemy why did they continue to dodge about?

Leaning forward in his eagerness for speed, Wentworth kept his eyes narrowed on those circling ships. Abruptly, he laughed aloud. One of them was scarlet, and it had the lines of his Northrup! He was certain again that Nita still fought there against the guns of the enemy. And she had downed one of the killer planes! He was within a mile and a half of the dog-fight when the enemy ship wheeled away to the East and raced off at top-speed with the Northrup following hard behind it. Wentworth swung his ship about, but he knew there was no chance of his intercepting the fugitive, nor of staying in the chase. Both of the planes were faster than his. His teeth clamped together. This might well be a trick, a trap for Nita, and he was helpless....

Doggedly, he clung to the pursuit, but soon the two planes faded away in the eastern sky. A grim fear clung to Wentworth. He had had time back there to see that Nita had averted an attack upon the stationary acid trains, but her work had been finished then. She should have abandoned the pursuit. A worried frown creased Wentworth's forehead as he turned his plane toward New York, lying smokily just upon the horizon. Within an hour, or an hour and a half at most, night would blacken all the sky. Nita might be ambushed by the very plane she pursued! Wentworth's lips tightened thinly. He was like a man with hands bound, forced to witness a vile murder. Nothing he could do would help Nita. True, there were fast planes in New York which he could commandeer, but by the time he could obtain one, there would be no chance of tracing her... Already there was no chance....

There was a grimness about Wentworth as he left his rented plane at the Newark airport, which kept his many acquaintances there from speaking, which killed greetings on their lips. He was driving himself to his search for the man behind the plague. He tried to tell himself that Nita was safe, that he was needlessly alarmed, but his memory prodded him. More times than he cared to think about, Nita had fallen into enemy hands. True, he had always managed to snatch her from danger, but he couldn't always win. No human being could always win....

Desperately, he thrust Nita from his consciousness, forced himself to concentrate on the search before him. If he could solve the murder of Christian Daly... There was no clear reason for thinking that Daly's murderers and the cholera-spreaders were the same—and yet Wentworth was convinced that they were. It was one of the Spider's hunches, the logic of his subconscious brain which he could never afford to ignore.

"To police headquarters," he commanded the taxi driver, "and hurry!"

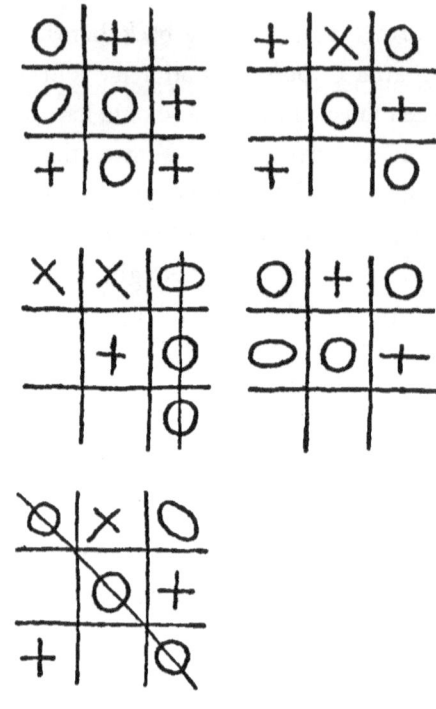

He drew from his pocket the notebook in which he had copied the designs which the murderer had inked on Daly's chest. He frowned over the characters. As he pointed out to Kirkpatrick, the symbols varied in shape. There were, for instance, ovals as well as circles, and the X-marks were sometimes crosses and sometimes had one bar shorter than the other. There was the additional fact that each symbol's position in the diagram might alter its meaning. Why else should they be placed in diagrams?

IT HAD been some years since Wentworth had attempted deciphering, but he could recall that where variants were employed—that is, several symbols representing the same letter, or the same symbol representing several different letters—it immensely complicated the task. He began a classification of the figures, regarding each symbol in a certain position as a totally separate symbol....

Before he had half-finished the task, the cab drew up before police headquarters. He showed Kirkpatrick what he had done, and the Commissioner smiled faintly. "We turned it over to Washington," he said. "They have the greatest cypher experts of the country there. Personally, I doubt that they mean anything at all. We have another set to work on now."

Wentworth's eyes lifted quickly to his friend's saturnine face and Kirkpatrick nodded grimly.

"There have been two more murders, Scott Francis, of the Rosco Steel Corporation, and Horace Todd, of the Hood Bank." He picked up a photograph from the desk, tossed it to Wentworth. "That's the layout on Francis. Haven't got one on Todd yet."

It showed a man's chest, pierced by a bullet wound which had struck the heart. The bullet had gone through the center of a circle in the middle of a tic-tac-toe diagram, and there were four other diagrams. In two of those, the circle symbol had "won." That is, there were three circles in a row and a line signifying victory had been drawn through them. Wentworth frowned, wondering if those three circles with a line should be considered a single letter, as he made a copy in his notebook....

Kirkpatrick took back the photograph, tossed it carelessly on the desk. "It means nothing," he said.

"I wouldn't be too sure," Wentworth objected slowly. "Did Ralds have an alibi for Daly's murder?"

"No, he didn't." Kirkpatrick dropped back into his chair, made a steeple with his fingers. "But we have only Carnes unsupported testimony that they even had an appointment. Ralds says he doesn't remember, but his secretary has no record of it. He says, anyway, that he certainly didn't keep the appointment."

Wentworth went slowly to the window, stared down at the deserted street, at the stone wall of the church on the corner. The emptiness was a mockery, and in the church, endless prayers were lifted that the cholera would end… Wentworth laughed shortly. There was a saying that God helped those who helped themselves. It would take more than prayers to end a man-made cholera epidemic. He forced his mind back to Ralds.

"Would he profit in any way by Daly's death?" he asked. "That seems to me to be the crux of the situation right now."

Kirkpatrick frowned. "Not directly. Of course, Daly's death throws his controlling shares of the subway companies into the open market at a time when those stocks are dirt cheap, because of the cholera… By God, Dick, we may have hit something there! A definite tie-up between the cholera and the tic-tac-toe murders!"

Wentworth wheeled away from the windows. "How about Rosco Steel? Scott Francis is chairman of the board. And Horace Todd, of the Hood Bank?"

"That isn't so clear," Kirkpatrick mused slowly, "though of course Francis is the directing genius of Rosco. If anything could make Rosco Steel shaky, it would be Francis' death. I'm sure the stocks were off on the market this morning. I hold some of them. Yes, off considerably. Todd? His bank's stock isn't on the market. Do you think, Dick, that perhaps…?"

Wentworth smiled. "I think you know your job pretty damned well, Kirk. It's just talking this way sometimes that you can dig up fresh ideas. And by the way, none of this stuff points to Ralds. There are a hundred others who could profit equally well."

Kirkpatrick got to his feet, put his hand on Wentworth's shoulder. "What a team we would make, Dick!"

"What a team we *do* make!" Wentworth laughed. "No, I will not be your deputy!"

KIRKPATRICK LAUGHED, turned away. "I'll put some men to watching Ralds privately, and we'll check stock accounts on Wall Street. Frankly, though, unless the murders are definitely related to the cholera epidemic, the plague worries me a great deal more, especially now that you've proved there are men behind it. We may have to shut off the city water supply."

Wentworth frowned. "In heaven's name, why? It would be disastrous. The sewage would clog up and spread fresh disease even if there were enough drinking fluids without the water. Won't the acid…?" He stopped as he saw the harsh lines of Kirkpatrick's face. He cursed. "The acid got through!" he cried. "It must have. Nita…."

Kirkpatrick shook his head slowly. "I know you and Nita did your best, Dick," he said slowly. "We had reports of how you drove off the attacking planes, but the trains were blown up by bombs laid under the tracks about fifty miles out of New York. Two companies of the national guard were almost wiped out—besides that one you already know of…."

Wentworth's knuckles whitened as his hands clenched at his sides. He had been so sure, so sure… He should have known that a man who could so cleverly estimate the Spider's moves when he fled ashore in the catapult plane would not have staked his venture on a single attempt to halt the trains.

He said heavily, "Then the cholera continues to spread?"

Kirkpatrick laughed harshly. "There are over thirty thousand cases reported. Every hospital is jammed to overflowing and we have turned all the public buildings into contagion wards. We can't bury them fast enough. Thirty thousand cases will mean twenty thousand dead within a day. Supplies of drugs and serum are exhausted, and…."

The police news-printer machine in a corner of the office set up an excited ringing, then began to clatter out letters. Wentworth and Kirkpatrick sprang to it, watched slow words jerk out on a strip of paper:

BIG EXPLOSION… BROOKLYN WATERFRONT… INVESTIG… FLASH… SQUIBB DRUG WARE HOUSE BLOWN UP… DESTROYED CASUALTIES UNKNOWN….

Wentworth turned to face Kirkpatrick and the countenances of both men were gaunt. They knew without discussion what this meant. The Master of the Plague was making sure that medications would not check the spread of cholera….

Kirkpatrick sprang to his phone, began barking orders to the guards who had been stationed at every medical warehouse and laboratory in the city. He ordered the men to search the buildings for planted bombs, and….

The police printer jangled again and Wentworth's narrowed

eyes saw more words of disaster wind from the machine. He looked for fresh news of the Brooklyn explosion, but found that a second plant in Queens, a third in Manhattan, a fourth in Newark had been blown to bits. He whirled to Kirkpatrick, saw from the grayness of the Commissioner's face, as he slowly replaced the phone, that he had already heard the news.

"There's nothing else to do now," Kirkpatrick said dully, "except to turn off the water supply. We'll keep the sewage flushed with fire hoses, supply bottled goods for drinking. We'll try to bring in new supplies of acid, of course, and medicine. We'll increase the guards…" He rose heavily to his feet. "Come, I'm going to the mayor's office."

Wentworth shook his head. "You haven't found Daly's secretary, young Bill Carnes, yet, have you?"

"Good Lord, no!" Kirkpatrick exploded. "As if there were time to hunt for petty murderers now!"

Wentworth nodded. "I'll see you later." He went swiftly to the door, stopped as Kirkpatrick caught his arm.

"Dick, I need your help in this. Help me smash this epidemic and the man behind it. Every criminal in town is on the rampage. There have been more killings, more robberies, in the last few hours than there usually is in a month of crime. The city is demoralized with panic and disease and the crooks…."

Wentworth gripped Kirkpatrick's arm, shook it. "I am helping you, Kirk," he said quietly. "I'm going to find Carnes."

"That youngster! He couldn't be responsible!"

WENTWORTH AGREED with a quick nod. "But he must have a clue to the reason for Daly's murder. Perhaps he can confirm our theory about Ralds. When I find that, I'll have the answer to the plague." Before Kirkpatrick could protest again, Wentworth was gone, a lithe, quiet man whose gray-blue eyes were masked to hide their fire.

Hot wrath burned within Wentworth as he hastened in his taxi through the city's deserted streets. Buildings were closed, blinds drawn as if, like the fight, they would shut out the plague. When men moved on the streets, it was furtively, with backward flung glances over their shoulders. Did they think that Death wore a visible shape these days?

There were trucks which moved with heavy clangor from door to door. The men upon them wore surgical masks, and heavy rubber gloves upon their hands. Even so, their eyes were frightened. Wentworth saw them carry a covered body from a house and drop it fearfully into the truck. All over the city, Wentworth knew, these scenes were being enacted. Already the formality and the dignity were stripped from death, and the plague was no more than forty-eight hours old. Bodies of the dead no longer earned the reverence of the bereaved. They were dangerous things to be rid of as soon as possible—bearers of horrible death….

The taxi driver turned a pallid face toward him. "Geez," he whispered, "Youse is my last fare. When youse gets out I'm pulling out of this hell-town. I don't want to die… I got a wife and kids to feed." He grinned weakly. "Want to buy a nice taxi, cheap, mister?"

Wentworth smiled faintly in reply. "They won't let you leave town, you know. The city's quarantined."

The driver laughed. "Yeah? Let 'em try and keep me here! They's hundreds skipping town every night, and I..." A queer, tortured light sprang into his eyes. He cried out hoarsely, frightened and the cab swerved, hurdled the curb and rammed its nose into an office building. The driver kept uttering, shocked, terrified cries. He pitched to the floor and writhed there, retching.

Wentworth was pitched violently to the floor, his forehead striking the back of the front seat. He crawled dazedly to the street, watched the cramped convulsions of the plague-stricken driver. What could be done for the man? The hospitals were crowded to overflowing, public buildings converted and filled, too. Without prompt medication, the man didn't stand a chance of recovery... There was a muffled shot and Wentworth sprang to the front of the cab. Then he stepped back, smiling terribly. The driver had had a gun. He had saved himself from the plague....

Wentworth strode with choppy, furious paces along the street. He could not use the cab, contaminated as it now was. He turned across town, reached Fifth Avenue and hurried northward. There were no taxis in sight, but the moan of sirens, police and ambulance cars, made a constant whimpering through the streets, as if they bewailed in advance the death of the stricken they bore away. The heavy corpse trucks with their masked attendants clanged along and not a few of them bore policemen in uniform, with drawn guns, who forced the men to their loathsome task. Abruptly, Wentworth halted. There, ahead of him, was a crowd!

The sight of a hundred people, crowded together in this time of plague, was a startling thing. These were days when men shunned their fellows as if each bore the scythe of death in his hands.

Striding briskly nearer, Wentworth saw that the crowd was filing slowly into the doors of the Hood Savings Bank. He checked near a line of men and women whose faces were drawn with fear. "What's the matter?" he demanded. "The Hood Bank is strong. You aren't afraid of losing your money?"

The man he addressed turned a furtive face toward him. "That's all you know!" he sneered. "It's on its last legs. The only man what could have saved it was Horace Todd, and he got killed."

The man shook a newspaper at him. "That tic-tac-toe guy…" Wentworth frowned as he went swiftly on along the avenue. Vaguely, an idea was stirring at the back of his mind. He shook his head impatiently. Somebody who had been trying secretly to get control of the city subways. It hadn't been generally known. Daly's death would give him his opportunity… A woman's scream broke in upon his thoughts. He whirled toward the sound.

The woman was old and, with her shoulders against a building wall, she clutched an old-fashioned, black purse with both her feeble arms. There were two men in front of her, one of them wrenching at the purse while the other tried to strangle her. The scene needed no explanation. Crooks were watching the bank on which there was a run and when someone withdrew a rich haul, he was robbed. But the old woman was clinging to her money with surprising strength, though her cries were long since choked into silence.

WENTWORTH WHIPPED an automatic from its holster too late. The crook who was strangling the woman lost patience. He jerked his hand from her throat and there was a glitter of steel as he struck. The purse came free then, and the two men pelted down the street. The old woman stood with her frail shoulders against the building wall, her thin, veined hands clutching at her throat. Then she crumpled to her knees and pitched down on the pavement, an abandoned heap of black rags. Those things happened with the flickering speed of light, between the time Wentworth's hand started for his gun and the instant it came clear. His lips twisted hard against his teeth, as he threw down on the two killers. The heavy forty-five crashed, jerking up with the recoil, dropped into line and crashed again.

The first man, the one with the purse, twisted as he ran, his hands snatching at his companion, the purse dropping. He was already dead, his legs flinging awkwardly wide. The second shot hurled the other against him, making a tangle of twisted legs and arms on the pavement. Wentworth moved stiffly toward them, gun in hand. Behind him, men were shouting, women screaming. But not one left his place in the waiting line at the bank.

Wentworth stood over the two men, a moment later stirred their limp bodies with his foot. They were dead enough, one with a convulsive hand still grasping a red knife. Slowly, Wentworth thrust the automatic back into its holster, his fingers went to a vest pocket where a platinum cigarette lighter rested. In its base was a mechanism that would print indelibly upon this dead flesh a small crimson seal that would brand these men as—the prey of the Spider!

Did he dare to use it? Back there in the line, a man had seen his face. Besides, he had promised himself never again to use the Spider seal while in his true identity. And yet... and yet the Master of the Plague needed a grim warning, needed to be reminded that the Spider still lived; that sooner or later, the vengeance of this man who was the left hand of the law would strike him down.

Only a moment did Wentworth pause. Then he stooped swiftly over the dead men and pressed the base of the cigarette lighter briefly to the forehead of each. Afterward, he went striding on. He was very lucky that there had been no police at the bank.

Behind him, a man shouted with almost hysterical shrillness. "The Spider! The Spider! That man was the Spider!"

Wentworth did not look about, did not hasten his steps, though the shriek of a police siren heralded the swiftly approaching forces of the law. There would be a few moments before they could arrive and by that time, he would reach the corner. Let him once turn it, and he defied the police to find him. He reached the corner, darted across the street into the trade entrance of an apartment building. He dashed up several flights of stairs, ran the automatic elevator down again and sauntered out through the front lobby. The police pursuit had already rounded the corner which the Spider had turned a few swift moments before—following a false trail....

AT HIS home, a few blocks away, Wentworth asked Jackson to bring his Daimler town-car to the door. The Daimler was not quite so swift as the Hispano-Suiza roadster he preferred, but it had one advantage—it was completely bullet-proof, and it contained a hidden wardrobe and make-up materials which would probably prove invaluable in the coup he was planning. He made a swift change of clothing—since police would have the description of the man who killed at the Hood Bank—and entered the Daimler.

"The home of Christian Daly," he ordered Jackson and settled back against the cushions with his eyes closed. He began to consider the happenings of the day, to analyze the diagrams of the tic-tac-toe murderer, but his mind was weary. The summer twilight lay like purple smoke upon the city and he realized that the long hours of battle that lay behind without rest, with scanty and hasty meals, had taken toll of his vitality. Was Nita still up there in that darkening sky, pursuing the fugitive enemy to the bitter end?

His lips twisted as he thought how bitter that end might be—a flaming death-plunge from the ceiling of the world. He jerked his head as if to shake off the thought, opened his eyes upon the deserted street through which he was gliding. There was a lurid glow across the northern horizon. For an instant it puzzled him and then he understood, and grimness cut deep lines about his mouth. They were the biers of the dead—the plague-ridden who died too swiftly to be buried, who could not be buried lest their very bodies further contaminate the earth and the waters....

Evelyn Daly refused to see Wentworth when first he entered the black-draped portals of her murdered foster-father's home. Having finally descended, she was totally different from the frightened girl she had been earlier in the day. Her dress was an unrelieved black and it made her face a startling white in contrast, widened her blue eyes to immensity. If she had wept, there was no redness now to betray it. Wentworth bowed with the courtly formality that was his….

"What business have you here?" Evelyn demanded, her tone bitter. "You tried to kill…" She choked on the word, pulled up her firm round chin, and repeated it quietly, "… to kill the man I love!"

Wentworth stood silent, smiling. His eyes, which could glance with deadly fire, were very gentle. He gestured toward the drawing room and, after a moment's hesitation, Evelyn went in and seated herself. Wentworth dropped into a chair facing her, offered a cigarette which she refused.

"Do you mind?" Wentworth asked quietly, taking a cigarette himself.

The girl shook her head, and abruptly the controlled dignity went out of her. She dropped against the cushions of the davenport, her head bent forward and slow, big tears slid across her cheeks.

"Oh, hurry, hurry," she cried, her voice muffled. "Can't you see…?"

Wentworth watched her and waited until the tears stopped.

"What I wanted to tell you," he said finally, "is that when I shoot at a target, I hit it. I would give you a demonstration, but it might disturb your servants. Really, Miss Daly, I did not attempt to kill Carnes today, but to prevent a policeman from shooting him."

The girl lifted her head with an effort, met his gaze with great, liquid eyes. "You mean that you… deliberately missed Bill?" Doubt was in her voice.

Wentworth smiled slightly. Drawing an automatic, he said: "I'll take a chance on alarming the servants. What would you call a difficult target?"

Evelyn Daly looked at the gun with wide eyes, her lip caught beneath small, even teeth. She flung out an arm rigidly.

"Oh, I do want to believe you!" she cried. "I do need a friend and Bill does… There, that rose in the vase!" She was pointing the length of the room, across the wide hallway to the music room beyond where, against the wall, a flower vase stood upon a grand piano. Scarcely had her last word left her lips when Wentworth fired. He did not aim—in the work to which he had pledged himself, there could be no such thing as aiming. He had trained himself to shoot accurately by pointing. Nor did his skill fail him. The rose leaped from its stem, severed between the flower and the fragile lip of the vase.

"You see," Wentworth said, "it would be difficult for me to miss a target as large as a man."

EVELYN DALY sat with her hands pressing stiffly down into her lap. A startled butler floundered into the hallway and she smiled toward him wanly.

"Nothing, Peterson," she said, "I asked Mr. Wentworth to show me how to shoot."

The butler's dignity was outraged. He stalked indignantly away and his stilted voice could be heard explaining to other servants.

Evelyn was staring fixedly into Wentworth's eyes. "I believe you, now," she whispered. "I believe you, but… Why should you care? What difference does it make whether I believe you or not?"

Wentworth had holstered his gun. He moved now to a seat beside Evelyn Daly and her head swung with his movements, her eyes holding his.

"I want you to know that I am your friend, and Bill Carnes' friend," he said. "I want you to take me to Carnes so that he can help me find your father's murderer."

The girl cried, "No!" Her eyes widened almost hypnotically. Then abruptly she was crying on Wentworth's shoulder, her slender body shaken by sobs. "We do… need help," she cried. "We… need it so."

It was a half hour later that Jackson tooled the Daimler into the street and sent it whispering through the empty thoroughfares of Manhattan. Evelyn had insisted on going with Wentworth to the hideout—a tiny apartment which, a week ago, she and Carnes had rented as their future home. They had planned to elope, to rely on Daly's forgiveness later. If he refused, well, they would manage somehow… It was to this place that Carnes had fled from the police.

"They papered it over just to suit us," Evelyn was saying, with a wry smile. "The living room was really smaller than we wanted, but we took it anyway. It's lovely, a creamy white with a widely spaced designed of cross fronds. They're in gold! We were… so happy."

She was crying again, silently, without sobs, smiling while

she did it. Wentworth took one of her slender hands, closed her fingers in upon the palm. "You will be happy," he told her gravely. "You must hold to that idea tightly."

His face was set harshly. These young dreams could still hurt him, though it had been long since he could dream so… with Nita. But he still could try to realize that dream for others. It was for such service that he had dedicated his life.

Carnes and this girl had done no wrong that they should be prosecuted. Neither had those other thousands whom the plague had smitten. A coldness crept through his veins, poured fury into his brain. How much longer would this damnable Master of the Plague be allowed to crush humanity beneath his iron-shod tread? How much longer…?

Beside him, Evelyn gasped. Wentworth checked his thoughts with difficulty, turned toward her. She was crouched back in the far corner of the seat, her eyes frightened, wide. He shook himself, drove the anger from him. The girl shuddered. "Your face," she whispered. "What were you thinking? You frighten me…."

The Daimler slid to a halt before a small apartment house of white brick, precisely like four other apartment houses in the same block. Wentworth helped Evelyn to the pavement. "I was thinking," he said quietly, "of the men who killed your father."

Evelyn laughed nervously. "I'm glad you don't suspect Bill."

There was no elevator and Wentworth followed the girl's quick steps up short, twisting flights of stairs. She was in eager haste. Up there, her lover was waiting. Wentworth's lips twisted a little with his thoughts as he followed her. She was fumbling awkwardly in her purse, standing before a door precisely like all those other doors. But behind this one, her lover waited. Behind it was her home-to-be, with its creamy wall paper and its fronds of gold....

With a little cry of impatience, Evelyn snatched a key from the depths of the purse, jimmied it into the lock and pushed the door open.

"Bill!" she cried. "It's Evelyn...!" She ran along the bare hall. "Bill... *Bill?*"

Wentworth's lips tightened in swift alarm. He reached the living room in two long strides. Evelyn had a hand braced against the wall. The arm wilted and Wentworth caught her just as she sagged to the floor in a dead faint. The room was empty, but on the parquet were a half-dozen scattered, dark spots and on the wall paper, between the golden fronds, were a half-dozen diagrams of tic-tac-toe!

CHAPTER 6
THE MAN IN SCARLET

WENTWORTH LOWERED the unconscious girl to the floor, loosened the throat of her dress and went about restoring her. As he worked, he glanced now and again toward the ugly diagrams that blotted the fresh wall—particularly the first, which showed a victory for the X-symbol. Always before, these diagrams had marked the death of a man. There were bloodstains on the floor here, and yet Wentworth did not believe Bill Carnes was dead.

To Wentworth, it seemed that this might confirm the theory that Daly had been killed to release his subway holdings. Now, the murderer wished to hold Carnes prisoner to learn certain facts about Daly's holdings, or to prevent his making public some incriminating information....

Wentworth cleared his throat and was suddenly aware that the air of the room seemed very dry and hot. His thoughts, too, would not run smoothly, but persisted in pursuing a numbing circle....

An oath rose to Wentworth's lips, but made no sound. He turned from the girl, stumbled toward the window, hands reaching before him. Ridiculous that the Spider should be caught in any such obvious trap as this. Narcotic gas. That was what it was. Narcotic... gas... The floor! He was lying... on the floor... gas....

VISION BEGAN to return to Wentworth very slowly, and that seemed to be far ahead of his other senses. Before he could hear, or even feel except for a numb tingling over his entire body, he could see that damnable face, bony and affrighting as a living mummy, peering down at him. Presently, he could tear his gaze away from those blazing eyes and see that the man had a great bald dome of a head and that, from neck to toe, he wore a scarlet robe. Wentworth saw also that the face was strangely without expression....

"Ah, my friend!" the man said, his voice high-pitched and harsh. "You were looking for William Carnes, were you not?"

Wentworth heard himself answering, his voice dull and lifeless. "Yes." That word had come from him without volition on his part and the fact startled and then terrified him. He knew something of drugs that left a man helpless, though in possession of his faculties—that robbed him of the will to refuse to obey commands or to answer questions. There were a number of them....

The man must have glimpsed the horror in Wentworth's face, for his eyes, burning and large, gloated down upon him.

"Now then," he purred. "You will tell me just what the police and yourself have discovered and what you plan to do."

Helpless to stop himself, Wentworth heard his lifeless voice talking, telling this man about Ralds and their suspicions concerning the tic-tac-toe murders and the connection between them and the plague.

Sweat stood out coldly on Wentworth's forehead, and he could feel the grip of the drug like a cold weight on his brain. The man bent closer, his great burning eyes fierce and menacing.

"Now then, my dear Wentworth," his harsh voice rasped, "you will tell me the best way to kill your friend, Kirkpatrick." He must have glimpsed Wentworth's desperate efforts to muster his will, for he laughed and the sound of his mirth was like a file biting glass. "Oh, yes, you will! For instance, I wish to know the name of Kirkpatrick's favorite drink—which he keeps in his bedroom—and what time it will be easiest to elude his servants and replace it with poisoned liquor?"

Wentworth willed himself to lie about those facts, which he knew as intimately as the routine of his own home. If he could only falsify the facts, this man or his henchmen would be captured at their work. Wentworth told himself fiercely that

The second man flung himself forward in a headlong dive!

this man was not only the tic-tac-toe murderer, but the Master of the Plague. His scarlet robe was a taunt....

"COME, COME, my friend!" the man snapped sharply. "If I have to give you another injection of scopolamine, it may prove fatal. Not that I'm concerned. I shall merely gas you again when I'm through questioning you, and when you awake a second time, you will have the pleasure of knowing that you enabled me to kill your friend. I think that will be much nicer than killing you, eh, Wentworth? For I can kill you any time. This way, I may enjoy your suffering. I fear I am a bit of a sadist, eh?" And once more the high-pitched, awful laughter grated on Wentworth's eardrums. The man in scarlet bent closer, hissed, "Tell me, now, how to kill your friend!"

Wentworth's lips and tongue formed the answers to the man's questions, but no sounds came from his throat. He had set his teeth hard upon his lips and was rasping them together, harder, harder He felt a blessed stab of pain through his tongue. The man bent over, struck him savagely on the face and the blow helped further to throw off the effects of the drug. Wentworth opened his mouth and laughed.

"Strike me!" he cried. "Strike me! Do you think you can make me talk that way?"

The man hit him again. Then he cursed, and from under his robe, drew forth a small, leather case from which he took a hypodermic needle and a small, opaque bottle. He thrust the needle through the rubber cap, filling the barrel of the instrument He laughed a little as he worked, his eyes never leaving Wentworth.

"It's too bad that I must inject you again," he chortled. "I would have liked so much to watch you after Kirkpatrick was dead." The needle was ready and he knelt beside Wentworth, picked up his arm. Wentworth tried to jerk his arm free, but his muscles responded sluggishly, without power. He felt the prick of the needle....

"Stop!" he panted. "I'll talk! I'll talk!" Could he muster false information now? His brain ached with the effort to think, with a heaviness that was intolerable. The subconscious portion of his brain and his memory was perfect, but brain-work was almost impossible.

"Talk!" the man ordered softly. "The liquor your friend prefers. The hours when his home may safely be entered."

Wentworth's head rolled sluggishly from side to side with the effort at thought. God, God, he must not die like this! He did not shrink from death, but he could not go without taking this repulsive monster with him. Wild laughter pumped up from his chest. "Kill me, damn you!" he panted. "Kill me... I... won't... talk!"

He saw murderous ire burn in the eyes of his captor, saw the man's whole body tense with the desire to plunge home that needle to kill Wentworth—after he had talked a while—and doomed his friend to die also.

"Kill me!" Wentworth panted. "I'll still have... to kill you... first!"

He saw the man leap abruptly to his feet and whirl away from him. There was a crashing explosion that hurt his eardrums and suddenly the room was plunged in darkness. The explosion came again, and a third time. Then a soft hand was on his forehead. A woman was sobbing somewhere in the darkness near him, and the explosion blasted once more. He recognized it now—heavy automatic. It sounded like one of his own....

"Oh, please Mr. Wentworth!" the woman wailed, and he knew that it was Evelyn Daly. "Oh, please! I can't carry you, and I'm afraid the gun is empty now. That man in scarlet—the man with the awful face...."

"Break out the windows," Wentworth whispered. Was he mad or did he hear the thin, wailing voices of sirens. Could they be coming already? He heard glass crash and the sirens were louder. But Evelyn couldn't have reached the window yet.... His conception of time must be entirely wrong. Yes, that was one of the effects of the drug, he remembered. The blessed freshness of the air washed over him, and now the girl was back beside him.

"Slap my face!" he ordered weakly. "Slap it, hard, over and over...."

EVELYN DALY was sobbing as she swung her palms against his cheeks, again and again. She screamed and a man laughed—the high-pitched rasping laugh of the man in scarlet. A great, burning anger swept through Wentworth and abruptly he was on his feet, groping in the darkness. His hands touched silk. He laughed crazily.

"Damn you!" he breathed. "Now, die!"

He found a throat and light blazed into his face. "Drop it!" a man cried, and Wentworth stared into the light that came from the window and down at his hands. He had Evelyn Daly by the throat. He released her, helped her to her feet.

"I thought I had... the man in scarlet," he said, his tongue moving thickly. "Accept my apologies, Miss Daly."

She laughed wildly, clung to Wentworth for strength and a policeman's blue-clad legs came scissoring across the beam of light.

"It's all right, officer," she informed him hoarsely. "A man drugged us and we were fighting him in the dark when Mr. Wentworth got me by mistake."

"Wentworth?" cried the officer. "The Commissioner has been hunting you for hours, sir. He wants you to call in right away to headquarters. It's something about your plane, sir. Crashed, I think."

Wentworth reeled and the last of the drug evaporated. His plane, crashed! Then Nita...? He got to a telephone in an adjoining apartment where a man and woman stared at him and the policeman with wide eyes. The Northrup had been found near Danbury, Connecticut, a flame-destroyed wreck. A broken wing with a number on it, saved from the fire, had identified it. There was no trace of a body in the wreck.

Wentworth gripped the telephone tightly in his hands. "You're... sure of that last, Kirk?"

"Yes, Dick, certain. I thought Nita came back with you!"

Wentworth dragged a hand over his forehead, through his hair. "No, the Master of the Plague has Nita, I'm afraid. But I don't understand the plane wreck. That broken wing shows they wanted it identified—and yet they haven't notified me that they have Nita, and I was just talking with the Master of the Plague...."

Wentworth's mind was still not entirely clear, but by the time he had finished telling about his experience with the Man in Scarlet, his brain was working swiftly again.

"Thanks for the news about the plane," he said finally. "No, I won't be down to headquarters. My plans?" He laughed harshly. "I'm going to find the Master of the Plague again and... turn him over to the police!"

When he went back to the apartment, Evelyn Daly clung to him. He thanked her gravely for saving his life and she smiled pitifully.

"I just came back to consciousness from my faint and saw that man in scarlet sticking a hypodermic into your arm. You were whispering to him to kill you...."

"Whispering?" Wentworth laughed. "I thought I was shouting at him."

Evelyn shook her head. "I saw your guns on the floor and I picked one up and shot it. I never shot one before and I had to hold it in both hands... I'm afraid I didn't hit anything."

Wentworth looked at the walls and smiled slightly, seeing where the bullets had hit. But there was no mirth in his soul. His thoughts centered on Nita and that burned ship. What could it mean? If the plane had caught fire in the air, Nita would have used her parachute... Evelyn Daly's hands were tugging at his lapels.

"Oh, Mr. Wentworth," she whispered. "Where's Bill?"

Wentworth smiled into her anxious face. "He's alive," he assured her. "If they killed him, they would have left his body here."

THE GIRL tried to smile but her head bowed and she strangled on a sob. She straightened and her eyes went to the diagrams on the wall. Wentworth felt her body go tense under his arm. Her shoulders came back and her chin lifted.

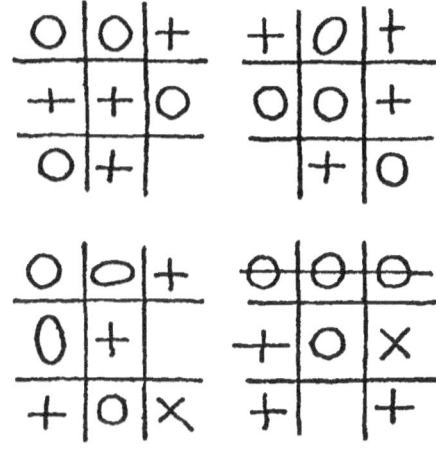

"They can't get away with this," she whispered. "They just can't!"

Wentworth walked slowly through the rooms. He found a pallet Carnes had made with blankets, found a few tins of canned goods and a loaf of bread beside it, all of them untouched. The Man in Scarlet then, had not been lying in wait for Carnes, but had arrived shortly after him. Wentworth returned to the living room and began to copy the diagrams from the wall. There was something queer about them which his partially drugged mind refused to recognize, unless it was... By God, the diagrams had been changed! There could be no doubt about it. Sometime after the narcotic gas had struck him, the diagrams had been changed, for he particularly remembered that the first diagram had had three crosses in a row, showing a victory for that symbol. He looked to the others, tried to detect any changes in them, but his memory was not equal to the feat....

It seemed to Wentworth as he made a painstaking transcription that these diagrams were a little simpler than those he had seen previously. He found, for instance, one symbol appearing in each of the five diagrams, the symbol X... Hell, this was no time for dabbling in cyphers! He pocketed the notebook, found Evelyn Daly's eyes fixed on him with painful intensity.

"Do... do you know what they mean?" she asked, almost soundlessly.

Wentworth shook his head. "Each one is different," he said slowly, "I'm half inclined to think they tell the next victim of the murderer. Otherwise, I can see no purpose in them. If they were simply a signature to identify the killer, there would be no need of a series of diagrams, and they would be always the same...."

He shrugged. "I do not even know whether the message is in the symbols, or in the lines which make the diagram. It might be either. Come, there's nothing further to be done here. I'll call police from downstairs."

Evelyn Daly went with him, but her footsteps were laggard. "I feel that I ought to stay here. Perhaps, Bill...."

Wentworth shook his head in determination. "You're going home, and then I...."

The girl faced him, her blue eyes deeply questioning. "What are you going to do? Will you find Bill?"

"If I can," Wentworth told her, but his thoughts had not been upon Carnes. It was time for the Spider to engage in the thick of the battle. He had given a warning there on the street when he pressed his seal to the foreheads of two dead men, and now... Wentworth's face held again the grim light which, earlier in the day, had frightened Evelyn Daly. It did not frighten her now. She seized his arm with both hands.

"Oh, let me help!" she begged. "Let me help find Bill, and…" Her voice rose, trumpeting… "Let me help you kill his enemies!"

WENTWORTH STUDIED her face. Dead white it was, with the blazing blue of her eyes. Before, she had been only a hysterical girl, stunned by grief. She was suddenly a woman, now, and her hysteria was gone. She would fight until the very end for her love.

"You'll get your chance to fight," he promised her. "Go home and when the time comes, I'll call on you. Meantime, you might try to work out this cypher."

Wentworth made two calls when he stopped to phone the police. The second one was to his home, and Jenkyns answered.

"Why no, Master Dick," the old man said, "I haven't heard from Miss Nita. Was she supposed to call? Is something wrong, sir?"

Wentworth said quietly, "No, nothing is wrong, Jenkyns." He went outside and looked up into the pitch-black sky. Clouds hung low in the heavens and there was the sultry promise of rain. To the northward hung the lurid glow of the corpse-fires. Fully an hour ago, Nita should have lost the trail, or… His lips compressed. He did not speak once while Jackson drove them to the Daly home, barely acknowledged Evelyn's farewell. When the car rolled on again, he swiftly drew the curtains and dropped his hand to a button beneath the front edge of the left seat. That part of the seat slid soundlessly forward, revolving as it moved, revealing a closely hung wardrobe in its back. Wentworth folded upward a mirror ringed with brilliant neon lights and opened a tray of make-up materials. Before he went to work, he caught up the speaking tube to Jackson:

"Take me wherever the looting has been thickest, Jackson," he said quietly. "The Spider walks tonight."

Wentworth began his skillful work then, swiftly coating his cheeks with a collodion-like material which stretched the skin, taut, sallow and shiny, over his cheekbones. It covered his lips until his mouth became a mere straight gash. Under deft fingers, putty built his nose into a predatory beak. That was all, except for the bushy brows and the lank black wig, but it changed the genial aristocratic face of Richard Wentworth into the sinister mask of the Spider. This was the man from whom criminals shrank as from death itself, whose avenging hand meted out swift, unswerving justice.

From the wardrobe, then, he drew out a broad-brimmed hat of black which slouched low over his eyes, threw a long black cape across his shoulders. He relaxed against the cushions, raised the curtains which shrouded his mobile dressing room and closed the wardrobe. The Daimler was speeding southward through the dark drives of Central Park. He glanced toward Jackson's broad shoulders, saw their tension. He could trust Jackson with his life. They had fought together in the World War, Major Wentworth and Sergeant Jackson, had saved each other's lives time and again....

The Daimler was on Fifth Avenue, which at this time of evening should be flowing with a river of luxurious cars, bearing gay crowds to theaters and rich banquets. It was empty. A single taxi ripped past with a roaring motor and the wail of sirens was a perpetual, sharp overtone as police raced to scenes of looting or ambulances rushed to aid the dying. Jackson opened the glass panel that separated them....

"All along here, major, they've been looting," he said, still using the war-time title he preferred. "They've got double police guards tonight, I see. The crooks have been stripping the apartments and the stores. Maybe tonight...."

HE BROKE off as a burst of gun-shots split the night. The Daimler snubbed sharply to a halt. Wentworth saw a policeman stagger blindly from a doorway where he had crouched. His arms were reaching straight up, his head wrenched back. It was plain that he was bullet-burned. As he stumbled, more bullets struck him, spinning him about, pounding his legs out from under him.

Now, at last, Wentworth saw the spurts of red gun-flame. The killers stood in a doorway—the entrance of a jewelry store. Another policeman was approaching at a dead run, his whistle trumpeting. Bullets met him, shoved back his head while his legs still hurled forward. He struck heavily on his chest and the whistle gave a last, wailing blast before he floundered out his life in the gutter.

These things had happened with the speed of motion picture shadows. Glass crashed as the crooks smashed the plate glass window of the jewelry store, bold now that the police were dead. If they noticed the Daimler, they gave no heed. What citizen would dare?

Wentworth was on the sidewalk, pacing steadily forward, a

gun in each hand. He saw one of the crooks whirl about and he shot with an upward twitch on his wrist. The man whinnied out his dying breath and the second crook, half-way through the broken window, pivoted to meet the gunfire. Wentworth fired again, almost casually, saw his lead hammer the man back upon the broken shards of glass....

The Spider stood briefly over the two men, his lips thin. Two gallant policemen had died that these two might loot. That they had later died, too, would not bring back two honest men, but perhaps their death might furnish a warning. He pressed the seal of the Spider hard to their foreheads, returned to the Daimler and pushed on.

He realized with a grim horror the meaning of his quick and easy discovery of looters. It was not that he was lucky in his hunt. It meant that the town was so rife with these killing marauders that a man could not move along the streets without surprising them at their work! Well, with the dawn, the Underworld would find something to check their bloodlust! They would find that the Spider still could strike.

Vengeance was not, however, his sole purpose this night. The plague had made this looting possible and there was a man behind the plague. If he were not directly involved in this plundering, then he would at least have a finger in the pie somewhere. He would not permit these carrion pickers to profit by his wholesale murder and not himself take a large share of the illicit gains. Perhaps, among the skulking jackals of the night, the Spider could find one he could make to talk. It would be better if Ram Singh were here. Ram Singh had a nice talent for making reluctant criminals confess.

Wentworth's thoughts flew to Nita, to Bill Carnes, snatched from the loving arms of that splendid girl. He thought grimly that perhaps he would not need Ram Singh's skill tonight…!

JACKSON WHEELED the Daimler off Fifth Avenue and prowled along the side streets. It had been nearly an hour since the encounter at the jewelry shop. The short-wave radio brought Wentworth the news that the Spider was known to be abroad; it brought also the information that the city water supply had been shut off except in the fire hydrants. In the morning, the fire department and the police would work together to flush the sewers—and to keep people from drinking the contaminated water while the firemen used it. Wentworth shook his head worriedly. There would be rioting. Profiteers would ask outrageous prices for bottled liquids. And nothing would be accomplished. The fire department could not hope to cleanse the sewers, to rid the city of that source of virulent infection….

A woman's scream, soaring and frightened, jerked him to the pavement. It came from up there in the air somewhere… He spotted the source quickly. At an open window, a woman grappled with two men, but it was impossible for Wentworth to get a clear shot. The bodies shuttled about. Most of the girl's clothing was torn off; her cries were prayers, frantic appeals… Wentworth flung himself toward the doorway of the house. For the moment, the window was empty, then he saw the girl lunging toward it. She sprang upon the sill….

"Wait! *Wait!*" Wentworth shouted. "Help is coming…."

His shout was drowned in the sobbing scream of the girl as she plunged downward to the street, turning over slowly in the air, striking on her head....

Up at the window, two men stared down. Wentworth's gun-muzzles swiveled upward, but he did not fire. His lips stiff against his teeth, he reached the door of the house in long strides. He slashed out the glass with a gun, turned the bolt and went leaping up the stairs. Shooting was too good for those swine up there....

Guns spat flame at him down the darkened stair well. He did not pause to answer with his deadly gun-fire, but went climbing silently toward them with the black cape flapping from his shoulders. His face was turned upward, bitter eyes questing for the men. They fled from the swift menace of his coming and Wentworth cornered them in the room where they had attacked the woman. He walked slowly toward the lighted doorway. He opened his lips and sent ahead of him the flat, mocking laughter that these crooks would know, the laughter of the Spider!

"The Spider has come for you!" he called, his voice stabbing through the darkness.

Within the room, the men screamed in panic. Their guns flung a hot flurry of lead through the door and Wentworth waited until it had stopped before he approached nearer. He played an old trick then, one that would not have fooled a smart boy. He thrust the crown of his hat, perched on the muzzle of a gun, beyond the casing of the door. Two more shots hammered at it, only one of which found its mark. Those, Wentworth knew, were their last shots. He dropped the hat, hurled himself into the room, his automatics level in his fists.

The two men cringed against the far wall of the room, drawing frightened arms tightly over their bellies, lifting a thigh as when a man shields himself from a hurled rock he cannot hope to dodge. Wentworth laughed at them, the same sinister sound which had thrown them into panic. One of the men dropped to his knees, groveling.

"For God's sake, Spider, don't kill us!" he begged, hoarsely, almost incoherent. "We was just robbing the dame. You don't kill people for robbing, do you, Spider? Honest, we was just robbing...."

Wentworth motioned with his gun barrel. "Over to the window, animals."

THE MEN screamed then, and the second one dropped to his knees also. The sight of them disgusted Wentworth. They sensed that he had come fully prepared to make them both leap from the window as they had forced the girl to do. Their cowardice was sickening.

"You have an alternative," he grated slowly, "How do you pay your share of the loot to the man behind the cholera? Who is he?"

The cries ceased abruptly. The men were trembling, inarticulate with a new fear.

"No, no. Spider!" one gabbled. "We can't tell you that. Honest to God, we can't. A collector comes around. That's all we know. Honest to God...!"

The one who spoke got crouchingly to his feet. Wentworth

eyed him sharply and the second man flung himself forward in a headlong dive for Wentworth's legs. Lead stopped him, pinned him to the floor, shattered his spine near the waist. He writhed, beating the floor, screaming, his fists almost at Wentworth's toes. Slowly, the Spider's gun came up to point at the second man's stomach. His lips twitched. The Spider did not kill men in cold blood, he had not intended to smash this man's spine, but if ever men deserved a horrible death, these did. He would have to quiet this poor wretch on the floor with a second merciful bullet. A curse was forced out of him.

"Damn you!" he cried. "Talk, or I'll—"

The unhurt man staggered away with up thrown arms. The window sill slammed the back of his knees and with a wild cry, he pitched backward into space. Wentworth half-sprang to the sill to catch him, then stopped, turning away with a twisted smile. Justice had been done…The man he had shot had ceased to scream. His breath whistled hoarsely in his throat and, even as the Spider's cold gaze returned to him, he shivered convulsively, once, twice, and was dead…Twice more the Spider's seal was imprinted and he paused a moment, downstairs, beside the pitiful remains of what had been a young girl. His face was wrenched awry. God give him the privilege of finding many more of these beasts tonight!

CHAPTER 7
"SAVE ME, SPIDER!"

THROUGH THE long, dreary hours of the night, Wentworth's car prowled the streets. This was not the vengeance he had planned. He had hoped to blazon the seal across the skies for the Underworld to see and dread—and so far only four criminals had fallen before his guns. He heard the police alarms over his radio, but always he was too late to reach the scenes of crimes. Three times, while the hours wheeled past, he called his home, but still there was no news of Nita. She was certainly on the ground long before now. Even a fresh tank of fuel would not have kept her so long aloft. Had she landed somewhere it was not possible to reach a telephone? Or had she… fallen prey to the enemy?

Wentworth shook the despairing thoughts from his brain, glanced about him. A milk wagon creaked by behind a clopping horse and its lantern was dim. Wentworth realized that dawn was in the sky.

"Not much chance of anything more, major," Jackson called back. "Drive you home, sir?"

Wentworth sat laxly in the tonneau and did not answer. A plan was beginning to take form in his brain. The robber had said that collectors called on them for a split of the loot. Suppose Wentworth were to take his place in the Underworld, commit a robbery and wait for the collector? It might offer a contact with the Plague Master. Determination stiffened his body.

EVELYN DALY

"Not just yet, Jackson," he said crisply. "Drive me down the Bowery and find a dark side-street to stop in."

Once more Wentworth opened the seat wardrobe and set to work on disguise. He kept the tightened, sallow skin of the Spider, but he changed the mouth so that it was loose and vicious, made the beaked nose lopsided, discarded the rough brows and false hair. His clothing he changed for a dilapidated, ill-fitting suit and cap. By the time he was finished, Jackson had found the dark side-street as ordered.

BILL CARNES

"I'll be here for several days, at least," Wentworth told his man shortly. "Keep yourself and the cars in readiness for anything. I'll communicate through Jenkyns. And Jackson, even if you have had the inoculation, don't take any chances on contaminated water."

Jackson twisted about in his seat. "Can't I go with the major?" he asked, hesitantly. "You can rig me up a disguise…."

Wentworth shook his head. "I'd rather have you where you can watch over Miss Nita when she comes back. When I get out, cut some doubles on your trail before you go home. I don't want the car followed." He stepped to the pavement, instantly merged his body with the shadows of the street. He heard Jackson call out after him, but did not answer and after a few moments, the Daimler rolled away. For half an hour, Wentworth remained there in the shadows of the street, making sure that his presence could in no way be connected with the Daimler. Then he turned and shuffled, hump shouldered, toward the Bowery.

Wentworth had known that the task which lay ahead of him would be slow and dragging, but he had not dreamed that the waiting would be so hard, that he would have to sit idle while the dread plague struck almost at his elbow and riddled the city with loathsome death—while familiar faces dropped from the crooked ranks among which he moved and in higher circles, too. No word came from Nita, nor from the man who must hold her captive—if she still lived. There was a stark fury in Wentworth's eyes these days which forced him to keep them perpetually hidden. There was a grimness to his bearing that he could not conquer. He made no friends in the Underworld dens which he frequented, but the criminals respected him. That was what mattered.

ON THAT first day, Wentworth had done nothing. But during the night that followed, he had crept into a wealthy home and burglarized the safe of much currency and jewels, riches hidden away by fearful owners, panic-stricken by the plague. He hadn't bragged of his haul, but that night he pretended to get thoroughly drunk and belligerently surly. It was a clear statement to his companions that he had made an immense haul

the night before. Now, there was nothing to do except wait—
for the collector of the Plague Master to come for the Master's
percentage of his loot!

Two fearful days later that collector came—days in which the
dead piled high in the streets, and the dying writhed in open
doorways because there was no one to help and no facilities. The
assault of the sultry heat that had blasted for days over the city
seemed to increase, so that even in the nights the pavements and
the brick walls of houses did not cool. The things Wentworth
had foreseen when the water supply was cut off began to mate-
rialize. A glass of beer sold for a dollar in the meanest Bowery
saloon and soft bottled drinks were the same. True, the police
caught a few of the profiteers at their filthy work and arrested
them, but the police had many tasks to perform other than fend-
ing for the poor in these murderous times. Even canned goods in
the groceries which had a liquid content went soaring to outrageous prices. Mobs were rioting, storming shops and shouting
with thirst-hoarsened voices. Children wailed in the empty
streets, hungry and thirsty, their parents stricken… or looting.

Wentworth was harassed. He must remain more or less
stationary so that the collector would have no trouble finding him when his stool pigeons—who operated so much more
effectively than those of the police—reported to him that a dour
newcomer had looted in the night. There were minutes when
Wentworth stood in the dingy room be had rented and shook
his clenched fists at the ceiling. There were times when he sat
slumped with despair in a saloon chair.

It was in his room that the collector finally found him. The fellow opened the door without ceremony, a brawny man with a seaman's roll in his walk, a man whose brows drew down low and black, above his eyes. When he banged the door open, Wentworth leaped to his feet, an automatic flying to his hand.

"What the hell do you want?" he demanded irritably.

The man sniffed, surveyed Wentworth's greasy garb from heel to head. He rested his hips against the wall. "My cut," he said shortly.

Wentworth sprang at him and laced the pistol barrel against the side of the man's head. He leaped back again and crouched behind the leveled automatic. "There's your cut!" he jeered, acting out his role of crook. "Now get out of here!"

The man reeled, hunched his bull shoulders forward and took a waddling step toward Wentworth.

"Listen, punk," he said, whispering with the tension of his rage-filled body, "I'm the collector for the Boss, and you pays my cut, or…" He left the word hanging in the air, wrapped his blunt fingers into huge fists, arms crooked.

WENTWORTH LAUGHED harshly. "I don't know your boss. Go tell him so. Now get out of here before I gut-shoot you." He took two short, pantherish steps forward, gun held ready in his hand, and the fury died suddenly from the collector's eyes.

"Hey, wait!" he gulped. "Listen, my boss is the one started all this cholera. He's the one fixed it so we could go around robbing without bothering with the police. We all pays him his cut, twenty percent of our take. So…."

Wentworth's expression of menace did not change. He spat deliberately at the man's feet. "Your boss don't cut no ice with me," he declared flatly. "If he wants me to come in with his mob, it's okay. I like a smart boss. But what I got is mine, and you nor any other mug gets any of it. See?"

Angry though the collector was, Wentworth had intimidated him by that prompt and furious attack and his unremitting hardness behind his ready automatic.

He went bellowing down the stairs and Wentworth heard him strike a man who blundered into his path, heard the man's unconscious body thud against the wall, bounce to the floor. Wentworth's lips twitched thinly, mocking at himself. All these days and nights he had wasted, waiting for a two-penny punk like that collector, who must wait until another man came to take his collections before be could report to the Boss that a man refused to pay tribute.

The dark hours of the night dragged past vacuously, as so many others before had done and, with the first gray streaks of dawn, Wentworth pushed himself heavily up from the bed where he had lain sleepless. His eyes burned in his head. He glanced at his reflection in the cracked mirror which hung on the wall and saw that they were sunken. Well, that would help his disguise....

He clumped down the stairs and out into the morning. It was cooler than it had been in weeks, but even so, the bricks that Wentworth's hand brushed were warm and there was a close mugginess in the air that clogged the lungs.

Wentworth frowned as he shambled, stoop-shouldered, along the Bowery. A sound of whispering pulled his head sharply about. In an alleyway, a score of men and ragged women were crouched, pressed dose together in the half-dark. Wentworth sensed that they were waiting, but for what he could not guess. AHEAD, ALONG the dawn-grayed street, he caught moving figures and saw that firemen were at work there, connecting lengths of hose to flush down the sewers, and abruptly he knew what these people in the alley were waiting for. They were waiting for water, waiting for a chance to wrest the control of the precious water from the hands of the firemen!

Even while Wentworth realized the situation that portended, the firemen moved on to a hydrant near the alley. He started toward them at a run....

While he hesitated, the battle was joined. The moment a fireman twisted the wrench that turned on the water the mob charged from its ambush, shouting, striking, screaming. A woman threw herself flat on her face in the stream of water that spurted from the hose, drank greedily like a dog. A man caught it up by handfuls and drenched his body, sucked it noisily into his mouth....

These people were drinking death. Death as surely as if the fluid they drank was a deadly poison. And those twenty were only an advance guard. The sounds of the battle drew scores of others from the sleeping buildings and from the darkened streets, shouting, crying for water!

The firemen were already overwhelmed, some slain, others fleeing. Within moments, the police would come with tear gas, perhaps with guns, to drive these suffering humans from the water that would kill most of them. Wentworth glanced desperately about him. He was beside a second-hand clothing shop.

For perhaps fifteen seconds, Wentworth stared at the broken window, at the tumbled clothing on the floor. Then he sprang toward it. Frantically, he dug through the racks of clothing and finally he found what he wanted. Incongruously enough, someone had sold his evening clothes to this second-hand shop. There was a long, velvet cape like those worn forty years ago. Wentworth whipped it across his shoulders, found a black slouch hat among the heaps of goods.

Two minutes after he had sprung inside, he emerged again, a figure of twisted shoulders who walked with a limping stride. Despite that apparent infirmity, he moved rapidly toward the truck which the firemen had driven and mounted to its cabinless seat. He flung up both hands, the cape swirling from his shoulders.

"Hear me, people!" he shouted. "Hear the Spider!"

Over the gabble of voices, the fighting, snarling anger of a famished crowd that found water at last, his clear tones rang. He shouted again and out there on the outskirts of the crowd, men heard and looked up. Their voices joined with his.

"The Spider!" they cried.

A girl got up on her knees, water dripping from her face. She said, "Gee, he's ugly, but… but, gee, I like him!"

A woman with a baby in her arms, said: "He's strong. He's *strong!* Help us, Spider!"

SLOWLY QUIET and half-calm fell over the hundred persons who stood grouped about the rushing hose. A man got slowly to his knees, dragging an arm across his mouth. Wentworth leveled a rigid arm at him.

"In six hours," he shouted clearly, "you will be dead of cholera!"

The man shrank back, his face warped by sudden fear, a trembling seizing his body. "God, no, Spider!" he cried. "Not that!" His frightened cries completed the stilling of the crowd and all eyes were focused on the twisted, caped figure who stood upon the fire truck's seat. Wentworth sucked in a deep breath and began quietly to talk:

"If some of you are criminals," he said, "you have feared the Spider... If you have murdered, or preyed upon the innocent, you have feared the Spider. If you have paid tribute to the Master of the Plague... you have feared! But who else fears the Spider...?" He paused and looked slowly from face to face of those who stood before him. "I have fought your battles for you. When men have tried to prey upon you—" He lifted his right hand and it became a knotted fist—*"I have killed them! Two nights* ago, I found men attacking a woman. Do you know what I did? Do you?"

He paused and there was a murmur through the crowd, a stirring like the wind. "Yes, I see that you do. One of them I threw out of a window through which he had forced the woman to jump. The other—I broke his back! These are cruel punishments, but wait—didn't those men deserve them? Has the Spider ever struck down a man who did not deserve death?"

He paused again and there were cries of: "No, no, Spider!"

He looked slowly over the crowd. The girl had crowded forward until she stood near the truck, her face uplifted in the dawn. She shuddered a little. "I do like him," she whispered.

"He's so strong," whispered the woman with the baby.

"What shall we do?" It was a man and his cry was almost hysterical. They were desperate, these people.

Wentworth studied them slowly. He had gripped them, but could he keep them from the suicidal thing they wanted to do, drinking the contaminated water? If he did, what could he offer them? More days of thirst, of trying to buy things to drink at prices none of them could afford. And in the end, what?… Would not the death of the Plague Master kill them in the end?

Wentworth shook off the heart-breaking depression.

"I have never harmed an innocent person. I am speaking to you as your friend," he went on, more calmly. "I tell you that if you drink this water, you will die. It is full of the germs of the cholera. Do you want to feel the agony of it in your bellies? Do you want to writhe on the ground with its cramping pains? Your faces will age overnight." He leveled a pointing finger at the girl, whose upturned face was strangely lovely there in the graying light of dawn. "If this girl drinks, overnight her face will be withered, her eyeballs will be puckered by the thirst of cholera. Then her flesh will turn blue and she will die."

The girl shuddered and covered her face in her hands. "Gee, I drank," she moaned, "but I don't want to die—like that." The men beside her shuffled their feet uneasily. Wentworth stretched out his arms.

"I beg you—go thirsty rather than drink this water. It means death. The Spider gives you his word…."

He dropped his arms and stood looking over them, and the question of their eventual salvation came back to him terribly.

109

What would be the end of all this? If he found and slew the Plague Master this instant, thousands would still die. It would be weeks before the city could be cleansed….

AS IF those people before him sensed his doubt, they began to mutter. A man forced his way forward through the close-pressed ranks, reached a bony arm upward, like the arm of Death itself. "Spider, Spider!" he called. "Let me speak, let me ask…."

Men gave way around him, they lifted him to the fire-hydrant and supported him there.

"Spider!" he called. "You call yourself our friend. You say that you protect us from killers and robbers. We believe you. But… can you protect us from the cholera?

"You say not to drink the water. What can we drink? A bottle of soda water costs a dollar!"

An angry murmur ran through the crowd. A man shouted a hoarse, meaningless curse into the skies. The girl was on her knees now, her face covered, moaning. "I don't want to die!" she whimpered. "Save me, Spider!"

The woman with the baby touched her on the shoulder. "He will help you. He can… a strong man like that."

The man on the fire-hydrant lifted his arms and quiet fell again. He turned and pointed at the Spider. "You call yourself our savior," he shouted, "then save us from this cholera. Lead us out of this city to safety…!"

Wentworth stood silent, feeling the pull of all those beseeching eyes, hearing the man's words as echoes of his own thoughts. They, too, wanted to know the end.

"Lead us, Spider!" rose the cry. "Save us from the cholera!"

It was the vocalization of the tacit cry that had burned itself into Wentworth's soul through years of the service to which he had dedicated himself. *"Save us, lead us, Spider!"* Yes, save them from peril after peril, from madmen conquerors and plunderers, from wholesale slaughter. It seemed to him that the whole city joined in the pleadings of these few scores, shouting to him with a transcendent pity, *"Save us, Spider. Lead us to safety!"*

Where would he lead them, carrying their contamination with them, spreading death wherever they went? But if they stayed here, they would all die ultimately. Was it not better to imperil a few thousands along the way, than that all the city's millions should perish? The girl stretched her arms upward, clinging to the fire engine. "Save me, Spider. Save us… please!"

The woman held up her baby. She was smiling, her eyes misted with tears and her face filled with trust.

A man surged through the throng and threw up a petitioning hand. "We are not cowards, Spider. Tell as what to do. By God, we'll do it!"

Hard resolution was growing within Wentworth while he stood there, listening to the cries and the wailings. The man leaped down from the fire-hydrant and came forward to where the truck stood, lifted up his gaunt arm. Wentworth stared down into his face. It was thin, hard-boned beneath taut flesh as if already the cholera gnawed at his vitals. But there was intelligence in the deep, burning eyes. His voice rose deeply.

"We who are about to die, salute thee, Spider! Will you stand idle and watch us die?"

It startled Wentworth to find a cultured man in a Bowery

mob, a man crying the ancient salute to Caesar of the gladiators who long ago had died in the arenas of Rome. But these people would not even have the chance to fight. They would be slaughtered....

Wentworth's head came up sharply; his hands stretched out while he gazed down into the face of the man who had challenged. "I will lead you," he said quietly. "We will march out of the city to the northward. In the mountains, we should find surcease from cholera."

His voice rose, soaring. "Many of you will die by the way. There will be hunger and thirst, and there will be death for any who disobey. But in the mountains, there should be purity and, after a while, health. I will lead you forth from the city!"

FOR MOMENTS after his voice had died, there was only silence. Then men shouted and women screamed in a hysterical joy. Wentworth stood grimly, staring at them. The girl was weeping silently. So they thought that salvation was as simple as that—a man to follow and a place to go? Did they think that only they could go? What of the city's other millions? He motioned to the man who had challenged him, drew him up on the seat beside him.

"You know as well as I that this is madness, but it seems the only way," he said. "How can we even feed them...?" He shrugged. "The course is northward. Send men into all these tenements to empty them. Send them south and east and west to tell people that the Spider will lead them from this plagued city. Seize all automobiles and put the women and children in them. Seize food and liquid supplies from the stores we pass and load them onto other automobiles…."

He stopped, leaned forward and pointed to men in turn. "Take the east side of this street for a block. Tell the people that the Spider is leading them from the city. When you find other men, send them to canvass the cross street, both sides, and the block beyond. Let them send still other men beyond. In five minutes, we march from here."

Men and women darted off into all directions, disappeared into houses. Moments later, others came streaming back. Within three minutes, the Bowery was jammed from wall to building wall with a crowd that extended for a solid block. Even while Wentworth looked at them, the crowd had swollen another half block—and another! He looked down at the men nearest him.

"You go the next street west of me, you to the east. Lead the crowd there northward." He repeated his orders about automobiles and food, sent more men still further east and further west.

"Cry the word to every house you pass. Everyone will not join you, but do not delay. Nothing can stop us if we advance together. The police will try. They may kill some of us, but in pressing on depends the life of the city."

The fire truck had been turned about and he stood now on its rear as he talked to the crowd, sending men to their posts. He knew that he suborned crime, that these men in looting stores for food would probably kill innocent persons, that death would march with him pace for pace. The sick and the dying must be left behind and at nights the dead must be burned. He must organize an incredible sanitation army, a food army. There was no other way....

He moved his shoulders heavily, constantly aware of the thousands who gazed upon him, who looked to him for leadership and for life. He flung an arm to the sky, turned, thrust his whole pointing body northward....

"Forward!" he shouted, and all along the street, to east and to west and to southward as far as the eye could see and the ear could hear, the cry was picked up and repeated.

"Forward!"

A city was marching out to death, or perhaps to life....

CHAPTER 8
THE EXODUS

ALL THAT day, the Spider's thousands marched, carrying everything before them. Hourly their ranks grew thicker as increasingly more people deserted the plague-infested homes to join the exodus. The subways were seized and hurtled their hundreds to the extreme limits of their lines; elevated trains, buses, street cars and automobiles all did their share. And in spite of that, many thousands traveled on foot, a great, growing army which filled the streets to overflowing, which crowded the city from river to river, stampeding to the northward and the hope of life....

It was noon when the first great cohorts of the Spider's army reached the quarantine line at the city's northern boundaries. A scant dozen men were on guard there and they watched the increasing hundreds who thrust against their bulwark with mounting anxiety. Wentworth knew that they had phoned for aid, that he must act decisively before that help arrived. Now, the thousands might pass the frontier without bloodshed. Later....

He went forward with two men at his back to parley with the guard, and faced leveled rifles with gleaming bayonets fixed. Wentworth smiled, and waved a careless hand toward the weapons.

"You can kill me," he announced quietly, "but you are here to preserve life, not to destroy it, and you cannot possibly wipe out the thousands behind me. The population of New York is moving northward to find pure water and a chance for life."

The leader of the guards faltered before the assault of Wentworth's direct gaze. He was a sergeant of the state police, and he was a brave man, but he looked beyond Wentworth to the marching thousands who pressed on through the sweltering heat of the day, crowding against the forward ranks now waiting at the barriers. Already those front ranks were feeling the inexorable forward thrust of them. The leader of the guards realized that their eventual advance would be as difficult to resist as the tides of the sea. Let the men kill all those that they now could see even and the dead would be pressed on against them. The gun sagged in the sergeant's hand.

"God," he whispered. "I can't stop you!"

Wentworth nodded. "Not you, nor all the troops in the state."

He lifted his clenched fist above his head, swept it to the north. Behind him, the thousands lifted their voices in a great shout. *"Forward!"* A bugle trumpeted amid them—someone had

115

caught it up in fleeing his home—and the shouts became a cheer. The State Police stood white-faced and watched them throng past, hundreds on hundreds treading on each others' heels, striped with sweat, some carrying bundles over their shoulders, others clinging to the sides of trucks and autos loaded with women and with foodstuffs.

The girl who had wept in the dawn went past them, walking with straight, graceful strides, her eyes unwavering. The other woman staggered beside her, hand pressed to her chest, but her head was not bowed. The girl carried the baby, riding it high on her shoulders, and their lips moved as if in song.

The marchers scarcely glanced at the armed men, their faces fixed with a glory—a terrible, urgent glory—*Forward, to Life!*

The sergeant turned to his men. "The whole damned city's marching," he exclaimed hoarsely. "Did you know that man in the lead?"

The private beside him shook his head, but his eyes remained on the marching hordes. "No, but by God, he was a *man!*"

The woman turned her head toward them and smiled. "He is a man," she cried softly. "His strength will carry us on!"

The girl laughed and bounced the baby on her shoulders.
THE SERGEANT nodded crisply. "It was the Spider. By God, I'd like to follow him!" He looked down at his uniform, at the badge on his breast. He was not a young man, Sergeant Mallory. His job and the pension it would bring were the only things he had to look forward to in life, to support him and his wife now that the children were all on their own. And yet the urge was in him to forget this uniform and the badge upon his

breast. When he looked at those marching thousands, there was something that caught in his throat like a sob. Marching in the hope of life, behind that splendid man. The Spider... the sob pushed into Mallory's mouth. He spun to face his men and had to swallow hard before he could speak. He brought up his right hand slowly and seized the badge, wrenched it from his coat and hurled it to the ground.

"If that badge keeps me from saving the people, to hell with it!" he said harshly. "If those people don't march, they'll die. I'm going to help the Spider!"

His men gaped at him. The first private pulled his eyes away from the horde. He grinned; then he ripped his badge off his own chest. "Want to make that an order, Sergeant?"

The sergeant's lips compressed to hide his own grin. "It's no order, no, but any man that doesn't go has no soul in him and no heart." He laughed. "Hell, yes, it's an order! Detail, *fall in!* Attention! By the left flank, *march!* Double time, *march!*"

They passed the ragged marchers with a grim steadiness which pulled many eyes toward them. A young man leaped into their path, brandishing a revolver. "You ain't going to hurt the Spider!"

Sergeant Mallory panted. "Hell, no, son, we're going to help him!"

The man with the gun stepped aside, cheering. Other voices caught it up.

"The police are with us! They're for the Spider!" Long before the police had reached the front ranks where the Spider strode, he knew of their coming. These men who joined him were sacrificing their jobs, but God knew he needed their help. This mob must be organized and leaders appointed to guard over them at night, to dole out food and watch water supplies, to aid the stricken and to destroy the dead, to enforce rules of sanitation. His heart lifted; his step was lighter. He would win through for these people because they trusted him, because he must. His cause was just and it would triumph....

He did not halt the march when the dozen State Police fell into step behind him. He clasped Sergeant Mallory's hand. "I'll see to it that you don't suffer for this, any of you, men. There'll be work which only disciplined men can do this night."

The dusk was gathering when finally Wentworth called a halt—a halt but not a rest. For him, at least, there could be no rest. The police and the few reliable men he had gathered around him went back through the crowd, dividing it into small companies, choosing the most likely man to head each group, apportioning the food and trucks and automobiles. More thousands arrived throughout the night and the work went on endlessly. The head of the march was ten miles beyond the city limits and its rear had not yet left the canyons of New York.

All along its length, fires burned, cook-fires and the biers of the dead. Abandoned buildings were filled with the bodies of those who died in the night and fires were set to them. The stench of burning human flesh clung to the refugees as they marched on the next morning. There were those who wept as they plodded on, and there were others who marched with dull and staring eyes.

But today, they marched in some semblance of order, the

companies grouped about the trucks and the autos which had been assigned to them, taking turns riding when the weak grew too weary to walk farther, seizing food supplies as they advanced, commandeering the milk trucks they met, seizing bottled goods from every shop they passed. The penalty for drinking water was death….

FROM THE roadside where they had been laid in the shade, those marchers who were stricken with the cholera, cried out for the others to save them, to carry them on or just to kill them. They cried unceasingly for drink and their pitiful wailings, too, became a part of the long trek. There could be no mercy, no pity for the dying, for their very existence was a peril to those whom they beseeched—a peril which all had abandoned their very homes and beloved dead to evade.

Vain as it was, the girl went time and again to those sufferers and gave them to drink. She was weary with a tiredness which gnawed at her bones. The thin shoes were worn from her feet, but an inner strength carried her on.

"If I die," she whispered to the woman, "it won't matter much. I'll never love another man. Not after seeing… *him!*"

The woman smiled, hugged her child closer to her breast. "My husband died of the cholera. They wouldn't even let me wash his face… There's a sick woman needing a drink, honey."

At night, those who were marching past at the time burned the sick who had died beside the line of march, and those who had drunk water were executed. There would be no need to repeat that salutary justice the second night, Wentworth knew, and thanked his God. His mouth was grim with pain as the order to fire was given.

"Murderer!" a man shouted. "You're in league with the Plague Master!"

The girl was crying. She turned on the man. "Fool!" she sobbed. "Fool, can't you see how it hurts *him?*"

Another man caught the objector by the shoulder. "If they live, they may kill a dozen men and women apiece," he explained quietly. "It's just like they were traitors to an army, or a spy."

There were others who cried out, too. If Wentworth heard, he paid no heed. Sergeant Mallory spoke to them, briefly, with a trace of a smile about his wide, solid lips: "If you don't like this army, go back where you came from. There's plenty of room in the city now."

To Wentworth, the nights and days alike were nightmares beyond endurance. If he slept at all, it was in dozing snatches daring the day's march when infrequently he mounted the fire truck which still led the exodus. He carried the whole burden of the march upon his shoulders and in the eyes of those who served with him there was something close to worship as he drove them on.

THE STATE sent companies of National Guardsmen from the north to halt the advance. They entrenched across the road-ways that the exodus followed and Wentworth walked alone to meet their commander. They talked in the colonel's tent. He was an older man than Wentworth, one under whom Major Wentworth had served in the World War.

They stood facing each other, an exhausted, unrecognizable

man in a dingy black velvet cape, whose eyes burned with the will which alone held him erect, and a soldier, spruce in his khaki, a strong man, too, with the steel of bayonets in his glance.

"The march must stop," he insisted. "Your people must turn back to the city."

"To die?" Wentworth hurled at him. "There are millions in this march, millions of human souls. Yesterday, seven thousand men and women fell beside the road with cholera, as nearly as I can figure. Today only three thousand fell. Don't you see what it means? They are marching away from the disease. They are winning the right to live. The cholera has a short incubation period, forty-eight hours at the most. Forty-eight hours after we leave the city, the last of those infected there will be stricken. Within a week, we will have left behind the last of those who were infected in the city. There will still be infection. Men can carry the germs in their bodies for several months, but once we have left it behind, we can isolate those germ-carriers. We can...."

"You can spread the infection across the whole countryside!" Colonel Brooks said coldly. "You will turn your people back, or my men will open fire."

Wentworth stood looking at him, smiled slightly. "Do you think that your three companies can halt three millions? They will walk you into the earth with their bare feet, hammer you to pulp with their bare fists. True, you will kill many of them, but there is a greater fear behind them than the fear of your guns. Colonel Brooks, if we spread infection in every city on our path—and we are avoiding cities—there will still be fewer deaths than if you turn these people back into New York."

Colonel Brooks shook his head sharply. "I have my orders. You will turn back."

"We will not turn back, Colonel Brooks!" Wentworth said it quietly. His hands crossed beneath his lapels and two heavy automatics leaped to his palms. There was a lieutenant in the tent with Colonel Brooks and one of the Spider's guns covered each man.

"If either of you opens his lips," Wentworth said shortly, "You both die."

Colonel Brooks sniffed. He opened his lips and Wentworth leaped forward, striking with the muzzle of the gun. The lieutenant whipped his sword from its scabbard and Wentworth knocked its tip aside with a blow of one gun, stepped close and slugged with the other. He stared down grimly at the two unconscious men for a moment. He began talking....

"I implore you, Colonel Brooks," he said, "to see this thing my way. Not thousands, but tens of thousands of lives are at stake. If you let us go through...."

He went on talking, while he bent over the colonel and swiftly stripped off his uniform, binding the man as he did so. He put his cape and hat on the lieutenant and sat him in a camp chair beside the table. His bowed head hid his face. The limp colonel Wentworth thrust into a shadowy corner. Then he swiftly donned the officer's clothing. He stepped to the door, jerked up the flap and when he spoke, it was as if Colonel Brooks stood behind him, ordering.

"Sentry, summon the bugler," Wentworth ordered.

WHEN THE bugler came, his eyes started wide at sight of Wentworth's unfamiliar face beneath the colonel's hat, but a gun in the Spider's hand—even though it hung idly at his side—prevented his raising an alarm.

"Sound recall," Wentworth ordered shortly.

Sergeant Mallory stood at the boundary of the camp, waiting, peering toward him. Wentworth lifted his clenched fist over his head as the bugle sounded, swung his arm stiffly toward the North and pointed. Mallory did not understand why Wentworth's signal should be given by a colonel, but he understood the meaning. He whirled toward the hordes.

"Forward!" he cried, and repeated the signal.

"Forward!" chanted the marching horde: "Forward!"

In the absence of orders from the commander, the soldiers did nothing. Wentworth saw runners start toward him from the entrenched positions and he smiled slightly, waiting. If these who marched were their fellow people, their own people, without orders from the colonel, but these were their fellow people, their own people. They would wait....

The runners came toward Wentworth at the double. Wentworth stepped inside the tent and let the flap fall, drawing the bugler inside with him. None would enter without command. He too, had seen Sergeant Mallory striding through the camp and only him did he admit.

"You were a captain during the war?" Wentworth asked.

The sergeant nodded, staring at the unconscious colonel in

the corner, at the lieutenant in the Spider's cape, at Wentworth in the colonel's uniform. Wentworth began to take it off.

"You're in charge of these companies," he said. "March them to the vanguard of our line and keep them there. They'll be a buffer against any other troops we meet. We can say that the march is in charge of the troops and is headed for a specified camping place." He laughed shortly. "Colonel Mallory, you have superseded Colonel Brooks!"

Wentworth doubted that he would convince the captains and lieutenants wholly of the replacement. He would speak to them, tell them that orders from Albany had been changed, that they would march with the horde… Then an armed man would keep at each officer's elbow at all rimes. He thought that he could handle the situation. Once more in his own clothing, he stepped out of the tent, with Mallory, in the colonel's uniform, at his side.

"Bugler," Mallory said sharply. "Sound assembly. Runners, return to your units and tell your officers to assemble their companies in their company streets."

The runners hesitated. One of them stepped forward. "Begging the colonel's pardon, sir, but Colonel Brooks…."

"Has been superseded," Sergeant Mallory announced shortly. "Return to your units and obey orders." He whispered to Wentworth, "I always wanted to be a colonel!"

The runners went away swiftly. Wentworth turned and shook Mallory's hand. "You can do it," he said confidently. "I think it would be better if I weren't by you when you face them all."

Mallory smiled with wide, firm lips. "I'll handle 'em."

Wentworth hurried to the head of his horde and an hour later, four companies of the National Guard passed at the double and took their positions at the head of the line of march. A lieutenant dropped back and clicked his heels before Wentworth.

"Colonel Mallory's compliments, sir," he said, "and will you join him at the head of the column?"

Wentworth nodded somberly, but he was gay. He had found a man in Mallory. Two days more of this march would take them to the place that Wentworth had chosen, and by that time most of the plague should have been left behind. He ordered the fire truck on which he rode sent swiftly forward. His mind was made up. He would leave Mallory, "Colonel" Mallory, in charge and go back to New York City. Somewhere there, the Master of the Plague still ruled, and the Spider's task would not be done until he affixed his small crimson seal to the butcher's forehead!

The Spider's lips' were smiling as he shot forward. Tomorrow, he would be able to join in a decisive battle against the Plague Master!

CHAPTER 9
DEATH FOR THE SPIDER!

IF NEW YORK had seemed deserted before the exodus, it was a thousand-fold so now. Infrequently, a bus hummed down Fifth Avenue and rarely was there anyone besides the crew upon it. The rumble of an occasional subway train, run to maintain the franchise, could be heard for blocks. Now and again, a scarecrow figure would show in a gaping doorway, or peer furtively from a window, but that was all.

125

Wentworth had realized that millions, literally, of the people had followed him from the city, but he had not realized that the desertion had been so complete. The plague must have ravaged wildly in the three days he had been gone, striking down the few who had remained.

He stopped the wheezing car near his apartment house and stole in through a back entrance.

Jenkyns opened the door promptly to his ring, stared at him haughtily.

"What do you want, my good man?" asked Jenkyns. Wentworth laughed at the startled widening of Jenkyns' eyes. "Master Dick!" he cried. "Master Dick. Jackson, Jackson! Master Dick is home!"

Wentworth walked eagerly into his penthouse, flinging questions at the butler and at Jackson, who quickly came to greet him. The news was not pleasant. Nita van Sloan still had not been heard from….

"I'm going back to the Bowery," he informed Jackson, "and this time I'll take you with me. You'll follow me night and day, or follow any persons who may follow me. But you are not to interfere, regardless of the situation, unless I signal you in the usual way."

"You mean the funny whistle, major?" Jackson asked hesitantly.

Wentworth nodded, waved a hand at Jackson's swift protests. Wentworth might not be able to give the signal some time. Why not let Jackson act at his own discretion…?

"I prefer it this way," Wentworth said quietly. "If I succeed in my plans, I may very well be taken prisoner by the Plague Master. That might suit my purposes better than being free, and I would prefer to have you as an—" he smiled gravely—"ace in the hole."

Jackson still did not like it. That was plain from the frown upon his wide-jawed face. But he accepted the orders and Wentworth knew that he would obey them to the letter. He told Jenkyns to get Commissioner Kirkpatrick on the phone.

KIRKPATRICK WAS very much pleased to hear from him, though he did not say so. Wentworth knew only from the crisp precision of his accents over the wire, from his mild sarcasm.

"I hear that the Spider has turned Moses," said Kirkpatrick, "and has led his people out of New York."

Wentworth laughed. "He seems to have quite a following… By the way, Kirk, any more of those tic-tac-toe killings? And has Washington had any luck with the code?"

"No, to that last," Kirkpatrick admitted more somberly. "And our chief suspect has been eliminated. Sam Ralds was burned to death last night and there were some of those tic-tac-toe diagrams on the wall. You haven't seen the message left at the time of Horace Todd's death either… But we still have other suspects. Walter Langford, for instance, would profit as highly as Ralds would, and his character will scarcely stand investigation either. And there's Carson—V.V. Carson, you know. His secretary reports that yesterday while he was telephoning he absent-mindedly played tic-tac-toe on his memorandum pad."

Kirkpatrick said that there had been two attempts to kill him, but that he seemed to bear a charmed life. He made light of it, though Wentworth urged him to be careful.

"I'll send Jackson for those tic-tac-toe diagrams," Wentworth said finally. "Will you please label the cases in which they were found and the dates? Thanks. No, I can't have dinner with you, Kirk. I'm going down into the Underworld districts and see if I can't find some clue to the Plague Master. I have a plan...."

Turning from the phone to Jackson, Wentworth gave him directions, and after eating a hasty meal, departed as he had come in, took the rattle-trap car again and headed for the Bowery... He thought the old woman from whom he rented his quarters stared at him curiously. As he trudged up the steps, and when he reached the door of his room, he stopped, listening, seeking the reason for that stare.

There were faint whisperings in there and, sniffing, he caught the unmistakable odor of stale tobacco. He smiled thinly. So they had sent a plant for him—the men of the Plague Master....

Turning from the door, he made his way rapidly up the steps until he reached the top floor, found the hatchway which led to the roof, crossed to the fire-escape. He was too old a hand at such hazardous living not to have insisted that his room have a window on the fire-escape.

His feet were silent on the rusty, iron treads as he crept downward, and, though it was daylight, no one observed him. This neighborhood, too, had sent countless thousands forth in the exodus. His room was on the second floor and the window was open, for the sultry heat which had depressed the city for days still held a strangling grip on the people's throats. Beside the open window, Wentworth crouched, waiting. The whispers within had died, nor was there any other sound. Wentworth frowned, staring out where the heat waves radiated from brick buildings in the sun.

Inside the room, a man spoke abruptly: "To hell with this. I don't think that mug is ever coming back. Let's go finish off Carnes and come back to this later."

The second man laughed. "It don't make no diff to me which one we kill first. Only I want a crack at this one. He socked me one on the cabeza."

"That's okay by me," the first replied.

There was a scraping of feet in Wentworth's room, but he did not hear it. He was hurrying rapidly down the fire escape toward the earth. His lips were smiling. This was better luck than he could possibly have hoped for. These men would take him directly to Carnes' hiding place!

When he reached the first floor, the men were still clumping down the steps. He had no trouble ducking out to the street ahead of them. Jackson would not be able to follow his trail further, but that was a risk he would have to take. It was more important to trail these men than to form contact with Jackson, which was purely a protective measure....

The two men swaggered out into the street, strolled leisurely. Wentworth had no difficulty in recognizing one of them as the broad-shouldered seaman who had attempted to collect the Master's double tithe from him. He frowned at that discovery, as he dodged through the shadows on the opposite side of the street behind them. The man had professed ignorance of the Master's identity and whereabouts.

A SHARP turn by the men he was following snapped him out of his preoccupation. They had entered the corner tenement on the opposite side of the street. Wentworth could not delay. He must know immediately on what floor and in what room Carnes was being held prisoner. These men would not delay their grisly work—Carnes' murder! Across the street, in the shadow of the elevated train structure-pillars, Wentworth sped at a hard run. He reached the door and ducked inside, his breath coming sharply, but without sound as he parted his lips. The footsteps of the two men were dragging upward carelessly. They had passed the second floor and were going toward the third....

Soft-footed as the deadly creature whose name he bore, the Spider sped up the steps in their wake. The men had stopped on the third floor and they were rapping in a peculiar rhythm which was readily recognizable as a signal. Wentworth memorized it even as he continued his climb.

He was on the third floor now, beside the door which the men had entered. His knocking would certainly bring suspicions, coming so soon on the heels of the other arrivals. But there was no alternative. By the time he could go to the roof and force an entrance by the window, it would be too late. He lifted his fist and hammered out the quick tattoo of the signal. The door was opened almost carelessly, but caution would not have helped the guard. Wentworth's foot was below the knob and as the door was unfastened, he hurled it in with a violent thrust of his leg, went through with it, a gun in each hand. The room was brilliantly lighted and Wentworth caught a glimpse of the man who had opened the door dodging into a closet to his right. It was only a swift flicker of movement in the tail of his eye, but it was enough. Wentworth's right-hand gun blasted and the man was hurled headlong into the closet, but he went face-first, with his hands thrown out wildly, and he lay with his legs still partly in the room, his toes drumming the floor convulsively as he died.

Wentworth had crossed the room in a single, bounding stride after he entered. There was another door beyond and he hurled it open, barged through behind his guns in the same movement. The door swung wide, then whizzed back too swiftly for mere rebound. Wentworth ducked it and the crash of its closing was like an explosion. He crouched, swiveling guns and eyes about in the room he had entered. Except for Carnes, bound hand and foot in a corner, the place was empty. There were no windows, and the door by which he had entered was the only opening. As he recognized that fact, Wentworth sprang to the door. Its surface was smooth and the cracks about its edges were only a hairline. Even as he attempted to open it, he heard the rasp of bar sliding home on its far side and knew that it was hopeless.

He crossed quickly to Carnes' side, unfastened his bonds, removed a gag from his mouth.

"What in God's name is the matter with you, Carnes?" Wentworth demanded.

Carnes smiled weakly, with a hint of the old boldness about his paw. "I had the cholera," he said. "God knows how I got over it, but I did… Would you mind, Mr. Wentworth, giving me some water? I don't think I can make it across the room."

Wentworth saw then that there was a lavatory in a corner of the room, a glass beside it. He frowned. "The water's turned off, Carnes, all over the city."

Carnes rolled his head against the wall. "Not this water. It comes from a tank on the roof and the man assures me it has about seventeen million cholera germs to each liquid drop. If that's possible, he's probably telling the truth. For God's sake, let's drink and die. At least, cholera is practically painless except for the cramps. I don't want to thirst to death."

Wentworth laughed. "He's a master of irony as well as of the Plague," he said harshly. "We can die of thirst and hunger, or we can drink his filthy water and die of the cholera."

"That's it, exactly," the sudden, rasping voice came from some hidden loudspeaker in the room. "Mr. Wentworth, your analysis of the situation is perfect. I might add that this building is filled with my men, so that there is absolutely no chance of your being rescued. Even while I talk to you, that door is being welded shut. And by the way, Mr. Wentworth, in case you should happen to think the police could free you—which of course they could, if they wished to and knew about your plight—they will find in the antechamber of your cell complete and conclusive proof that you are the Spider. I won't bore you with details of that evidence, but it is quite, quite complete!"

CHAPTER 10
NITA'S CHOICE

T HAT MOCKING laughter echoed also in the ears of Nita van Sloan, a score of miles away from the scene of Wentworth's torture. For the Man in Scarlet did not speak from the next room, as it had seemed, but over a telephone hook-up with a loudspeaker attachment, connecting the escape-proof cell with his hidden headquarters on Long Island. And Nita, a prisoner, though unbound, sat near the scarlet-clad figure of the man.

As he finished jeering at Wentworth, he threw a tumbler which disconnected the telephone hook-up and turned the hard-boned mask of his face toward her.

"There, Miss van Sloan," came the harsh, high-pitched voice. "Did I not predict that he would walk into that trap like any fool mouse after the cheese? One need only supply the right bait to trap even the Spider, my dear!"

Nita no longer wore the dark silk suit in which she had been clad when she had flown on that ill-fated trip with Wentworth. Her robe was of that exquisite soft blue which she loved so much.

"I do not think that I shall repent my bargain, my dear," he said. "If those fools who shot you down had killed you, I should have had them pulled slowly to bits with red-hot pincers."

"You will do, of course, whatever you have made up your mind to do," she acknowledged calmly. "You should have learned by now that you can't goad me."

133

The man chuckled and his hands reached out. But they did not touch Nita, though the longing to do so was in the slender, flexible fingers and in those burning eyes.

"No, no," he whispered. "I will never touch you until you come willingly into my arms, my dear. And you will do that very soon, I think. Very, very soon—"

Nita's eyes met his without flinching, without wavering, nor did she shrink one inch from those repulsive fingers.

"You are more than mistaken," she said scornfully. "You are a fool!"

She turned away, hate and anger burning within her, but she took only a step before the man's hand closed on her wrist and whirled her around to face him.

"I regret the violence, Miss van Sloan," he said hissingly, "but you were unmannerly in leaving, and I never could abide impoliteness. I will bother you to accompany me to the phone again. Miss van Sloan. I have decided to talk with your lover's jailers!"

The Man in Scarlet threw the telephone switch. "How is my prisoner behaving?" he asked gently.

A hoarse voice answered him. "He seems to be playing some game, master. It looks like tic-tac-toe from where we are."

"I want my prisoner to be comfortable." The voice of the Man in Scarlet was a harsh purr. "Turn on the heat at full force!"

Nita's even teeth closed on her lip. It was inhuman!

"Report to me every fifteen minutes," Nita's captor instructed.

Nita choked back the strangled sob that rose to her throat. God in heaven give her strength, for presently she knew this creature would present her a problem for solution. When he had satisfied his cruelty through torturing Dick and that other poor boy, he would give her a choice—Dick's death or her own passive slavery.

NITA'S FACE and poise showed not one atom of the heart-breaking struggle within her, though the pallor of her cheeks might have betrayed her, had she not been pale ever since her capture. The Man in Scarlet strolled slowly up and down the room, now and then lifting his gaunt arms and slender hands so that his silken sleeves draped back more gracefully.

Minutes dragged past and the first quarter hourly report came in over the telephone.

"And how are my prisoners doing?"

"Carnes has stripped down," the answer came hoarsely. "He's lying on the floor panting. This Spider guy ain't even moved. He's sweating like a horse, but he just sits there on the floor playing that damned game."

"Turn on still more heat!" raged the Plague Master.

The jailer faltered. "Master, there ain't no more. They got it all!"

"Keep it up!" the Master ordered. He sprang from his seat and strode restlessly back and forth. Nita clasped her hands in her lap, and kept her eyes lowered.

The quarter hours dragged on, and though Carnes was suffering extreme exhaustion, Wentworth had persistently worked on the codes except occasionally when he rose to get water from the lavatory and bathe Carnes' suffering body with the liquid neither of them dared drink. When twenty of those fifteen-minute reports had been made, the jailer reported that Wentworth had stopped the "game."

"He's stretched out flat on his back, smiling at the ceiling," the man grated. "He acts like he'd won a million dollars at craps."

The Plague Master pursed his lips, nodded slowly. "Five hours is a very short time for solving my cypher. Apparently, I gave him his first opportunity to work on it." He hung up the phone, turned his bald head toward Nita. "I'm afraid the solution comes a bit too late to be of much service," he chortled. "Well, my dear, let us retire and get a bit of rest. By this time tomorrow, your lover should be feeling a few hunger pangs. But we won't hurry him, nor you, my dear." He rose and bowed with a grotesque grace. "I give you good-night, Miss van Sloan!"

NITA ROSE wearily to her feet. She was past thinking because of her fatigue, past anything but suffering… She was half-way across the room when the buzzer of the phone whirred venomously as a rattle snake. She turned about sharply and saw that the Plague Master was hurrying back to the instrument. He caught up the receiver, dropped into the chair.

"Well?… What do you say? The police? But how in the name of the devil…? Of course, I can send reinforcements, within a few moments, but I may decide to let you abandon the place—in which case you will leave by the tunnel. Yes, hold them off for a few minutes. You should have grenades and ammunition enough for that."

The Master let the receiver hang and twisted about on his chair to face Nita, who stood straight and still in the middle of the room.

"Miss van Sloan," said her captor slowly, "with his customary foresight, your lover apparently arranged for a police investigation of his continued absence. They have located one of my smaller headquarters, where I have him prisoner. I think I have explained the situation to you pretty thoroughly. One of two things can be done. I can leave evidence which will prove he is the Spider… and hence achieve his death in the electric chair. Or I can adjust matters so that when his room is forced, he and everyone else will be blown sky-high."

He chuckled, rubbing his long-fingered hands drily together. "Fortunately, I am able to offer still another alternative. While the forces I have in the building at present aren't powerful to defeat the police, I can send others to drive them away. In that case, Wentworth would continue to live in the cell, or…" He looked at her sharply… "I could have him brought here for a while, and afterward released on parole, or shall we say, in hostage?"

Nita was staring straight before her with a fixity that sent pains through her eyeballs. The tension was in her whole body and she could not ease it. She felt that her face was hard and stiff, too.

"It is for you to say, my dear," the Master purred. "Shall I release him and bring him here… for a while, and then release him with yourself as hostage?"

Nita swallowed and tried to part her lips, but no sound came from them. The Plague Master came to his feet, moved slowly near her, lifting his hands so that the silken sleeves slid back from the gaunt forearms.

"My dear," he said persuasively. "I will do you a signal honor. I have said that I will not touch you unless you come to me of your own volition. I will do even more than that. If you so desire, *I will marry you!*"

LAUGHTER BUBBLED from Nita uncontrollably. It burst apart her sealed lips, shook her body so that she staggered.

"Beware, woman!" he thundered, "lest I withdraw the honor, and make you merely my slave!"

Nita clasped her hands before her, white fingers writhing tightly together. Oh, they were talking, talking while the police fought into that house so far away, where their success meant Dick's death surely—whether they found him or only the evidence against him… She lifted her hands before her as if she prayed.

"Speak now!" the Master commanded harshly. "If you will marry me, I will spare your lover's life! Answer, woman!"

Nita's hands dropped limply.

"Yes," she answered clearly.

"You will marry me?"

Nita's head tossed back, her lips warping in that smile. "Yes, oh yes. I give you my promise. Now, keep yours…."

The words were stopped on her mouth by the man's kiss. She felt his arms about her soft body like thin wires of steel, felt those long, limber fingers caress her shoulder….

His breath was harsh in his throat when abruptly he whirled away and ran to the phone. Nita staggered back against the piano and with the back of her hand scrubbed her mouth. A shudder shook her whole body, but there was no faltering in the clear courage of her eyes. If she could buy Dick's life, she would count any cost light… She hoped she would. God must make it light. God must help a woman in her sacrifice….

CHAPTER 11
DEATH'S HARVEST

THE SOUNDS of the conflict outside his cell penetrated only dimly to Wentworth, but he heard them and his eyes lighted, his lips smiled to the news it brought. He had given Jackson positive instructions not to act without his orders, but Jackson, he knew, would consider that his prolonged absence voided previous instructions. He had been waiting for the police, longing for them despite the warning of the Plague Master that their coming would expose conclusive evidence that he was the Spider.

Ah, the shooting and the cries had suddenly died, there beyond the wall. How much longer would it be before help came? Wentworth remembered his automatics and drew each one in turn, carefully checked the loading and safety. He was fairly sure that police would open that welded door, but it was well to be prepared… Once more the hissing of an electric flame came, this time eating away the barrier which imprisoned them. Wentworth shook Carnes's shoulder a little, grinned down at him.

Then he saw the door sway and got carefully to his feet, took two steps to the left of where Carnes lay, drawing his guns. The door crashed inward to the floor and a man in a cop's blue

A violent blow crashed on the back of

Wentworth's head. He had been tricked!

uniform staggered back from the heat, ducked his head and plowed into it.

"Come on out, you two!" he grinned. "You must be about done by now in this oven!"

Wentworth laughed and shoved his guns back into their holsters, turned to help Carnes to his feet. A violent blow crashed on the back of his head and his brain exploded in red-and-white lights. He realized in the ghastly moment before he subsided into senselessness that he had been tricked. That man in police clothes had blackjacked him!

CONSCIOUSNESS RETURNED to the Spider while he was being half-led, half-carried along a long, dark hallway. Many men were with him, but they walked without conversation and they trod lightly. Within the first few moments, Wentworth discovered that his arms were bound together behind him and that the men with him were not police.

It was apparent in the furtiveness of their tones—even before he began to make out distinct words. Abruptly, light blazed into his eyes and when he could see again, he stood before a raised dais on which sat the Man in Scarlet! And, at his feet, with her head resting on his knees, and with his hand touching her bared shoulder, sat... Nita van Sloan!

The Man in Scarlet chuckled. "What, lovers, and you do not speak? Come, come, Spider Wentworth, I thought better of your manners than that!"

WENTWORTH SMILED gently. "I thought better of your abilities, my dear sir, than to think it would be necessary for you to coerce a lady, even though she is so far above you!"

The man thumped to his feet, scarlet robe swirling as he strode forward to tower over Wentworth from the edge of the dais. "If I had not promised to spare you life…!"

He threw back his head sharply and laughed. "We marry tonight, the lady and I, and tomorrow you may go free. The lady will be hostage for your proper conduct!" He walked back and drew Nita to her feet, stooped to kiss her still lips.

Wentworth rocked with the rage that pounded in him and two more men seized his arms and wrists. He locked his lips upon the surging hatred, pulled his eyes away from Nita through long moments while he fought for control.

But Wentworth had not yet despaired. There was still a slim hope that Jackson might bring help. Of course, that attack while Wentworth had been prisoner in the sealed cell was a ruse. But maybe Jackson had trailed him still farther. If he had, if he had….

Wentworth puckered his lips and whistled softly the weird tune which was the signal agreed upon between them. The response was like a bolt of lightning!

From somewhere overhead, a submachine gun stammered and men's shrill screams drowned out its staccato chatter. The guards flung away to right and left of Wentworth and revolvers began to speak, seeking out the gunman. The Plague Master had snatched Nita in a long arm and he held her before him as he backed toward the wall, leveling a long-barreled automatic with his free hand. The man's face remained impassive, but the blazing hatred in his eyes gave Wentworth warning, even before the

Wentworth hurled himself behind the dais as the monster fired at him!

muzzle swung toward him. He hurled himself below the edge of the dais for protection, heard hot lead scream over his head....

A MURDEROUS fury was upon him. That monster was fleeing, carrying Nita with him! If he escaped, his men would spread to the four corners of the continent sowing the germs of the fearful plague, furthering his dreadful conquest.

Wentworth surged to his feet. Men of the Plague Master lay scattered on the floor, weltering in death. A few had escaped to the hallways and, as Wentworth watched, one of them leveled a revolver at him and fired. A numbing shock hurled Wentworth backward upon the edge of the dais, but he was on his feet again instantly. The lead had found a billet in his body—where he did not know—but his rage was a volcano within him. His shoulders swelled; he set his legs and, with a violent wrench, tore his hands free of the ropes which bound them. Skin was ripped from his fingers and wrists. He had felt a bone snap in his left hand, but he was free, free....

With a shout that was terrible in its anger, he hurled himself toward the dead, and snatched up guns. That man who had wounded him fired another shot, but whether from fear or excitement, it went wild. The Spider fired and his shot sped true.

"Jackson!" he shouted. "Get outside. Stop the man in scarlet!"

"Down the hallway, sir!" Jackson shouted back. "You can get out faster than I can. I'm tied in a rope sling. It's the only way I could use the gun...."

Wentworth pelted toward the hallway. Strangely, instead of plunging through the doorway, he hit its edge with his shoulder, reeled across the corridor and would have fallen but that his gun-hand, rigidly outthrust, caught his weight. He leaned there a moment, breathing deep and noisily, looking down at his side.

There was a spreading stain there, below the short ribs. Wentworth took off his belt, and drew it tightly over the wound. Agonizing pains shot through his body, but when it was done, he could stagger on to the pursuit….

He was only halfway down the hall when Jackson overtook him, threw a strong arm about his body. "You're wounded, Major!" he cried. "Stop and let me…."

"Stop hell!" Wentworth rasped. "The Plague Master is getting away. Jackson, he's got Nita… Nita…!"

Out of the darkness ahead, Nita's voice lifted in answer for a moment; then it was choked off. A motor roared, dwindled again into the distance.

Wentworth gasped Nita's name at every breath, and his breath was strained and scant, broken by coughing that seemed to tear flesh. Jackson steered him to an automobile, got him into it and started the car rolling. Wentworth coughed again. "Touched the lung," he choked. "Bullet touched lung…."

The car bellowed on a short driveway, skidded into a road and began to gather momentum. "Don't know this section too well, sir," Jackson said. "We might lose them…."

Wentworth laughed, broke with a cough. Don't try to follow. Go to Manhattan. Riverside Towers."

JACKSON PEERED at him anxiously. Riverside Towers was Miss Nita's residence. Could the major's mind be wandering because of the wound? Jackson's lips tightened. The major needed medical attention—and needed it at once. To hell with this chase. Jackson had no thoughts of service to humanity. His service and devotion was for one man.

Wentworth braced himself solidly in the corner of the cushions, looked about him with swimming vision. But the rush of air was fighting the giddiness from his wound.

"Jackson," he shouted clearly. "Damn your eyes, I said Manhattan, and Riverside Towers! You're heading north, instead of west."

Jackson's jaw was stubborn, but he flashed a look at Wentworth's set face, at the fine, strong line of his chin and the direct eyes. By God, the major meant what he said! He couldn't be so badly wounded....

Jackson grinned. "Right you are. Major!" He spun the car to the left at the next crossroad, trod the accelerator to the floor. Wentworth began to talk.

"Cracked that damned code wide open," he said, speaking slowly as if he were being careful of every word. "And so I know where to look for the Master of the Plague, Jackson. He always was crazy about Miss Nita. He had even taken an apartment in the same building, rather secretly, some time ago. Made an effort at disguise when I saw him. Fool. As if he could trick a man who created disguise...."

JACKSON, EYES fixed on the road which was sliding under the wheels at better than seventy miles an hour, said merely, "Yes, sir!"

"We're going after a dead man, Jackson, a man everybody thinks is dead. But he's very much alive right now..." Wentworth's breath gusted out through his teeth. He fought down the cough. "Alive right now, but he won't be long.

"You see, Jackson, every one of those code messages was the name of a victim, or a clue to him, and they were in trick codes, with double substitutions and plenty of variants and nulls. But the guilty man? Really a very simple code, and only one substitution, so if every other diagram went uninterrupted this one at least would be understood. Yes, he wanted to be sure that everyone thought him dead." His head bowed, his thoughts misty. "Poor Evelyn Daly...."*

---

* AUTHOR'S NOTE: Richard Wentworth explained his solving of the codes in this way: Taking all of the messages, he found that eleven variations of the simple circle and cross-mark were used. He figured further that if each of these symbols had a different meaning in each of the nine rectangles, it would give ninety-nine letters, which was far too many for the English, twenty-six-letter alphabet. Yet the eleven variations were not enough in themselves, so he figured finally that by dividing the nine rectangles into three rows of three each and giving a variation a different meaning, not in each square, but in each row, he would have only thirty-three characters which was much closer to the correct total of twenty-six. Studying the diagrams, he found a great number of simple circles and cross-marks, occurring in such sequences that it made it impossible for him to believe that they had a meaning, thus three simple circles in a straight sequence would mean say, three E's, or three T's. The English language does not have such sequences. Logic showed him that it would be impossible to make sequences of letter-symbols alone in the diagrams, and still make them seem games of tit-tat-toe, so he assumed the presence of nulls and decided, as a first try, to call nulls

whatever symbols appeared most frequently. As an examination will show, this was clearly the simple circle and the plain cross. So much for the analysis of the diagrams, in its successful form. I say nothing of the attempts to find meaning in set sequences of characters, in the varying lengths and shapes of the rectangles and of the lines which divided them. All those were eliminated finally by trial-and-error method through a sheer inability to make sense of them ... For the actual deciphering of the code: Wentworth, as we know, was convinced that the diagrams gave the name of the *next victim*. Working from this basis, he finally found one diagram which gave a name, that of Ralds, as he explained to Jackson. If you will turn back to the diagram found on the wall in Carnes' apartment, and compare it with the key given at the end of this footnote, you will be able to read the message "Die Raids!" Others of the warnings were not so simple, but because the first three letters invariably made sense when the Raids key was applied, Wentworth finally decided that those first three letters were in themselves a key. For instance in the first diagrams, found on the chest of Christian Daly, the first three letters formed the word SOT. The subsequent letters were a jumble, thus JCLUC. Wentworth deduced that the word SOT at the beginning of the

code message meant that in the next letter following, the letter J would be taken from a substitution alphabet in which A equals S, B equals T, C equals U and so on; that the second letter following the word SOT, in this case C, would be taken

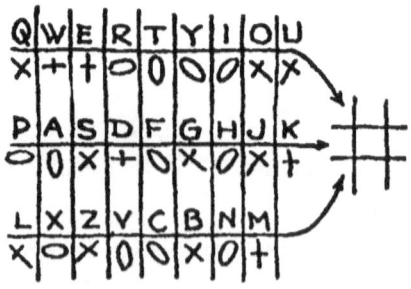

Note: O and + are nulls.

"Another thing, Jackson. When the Man in Scarlet knocked me out with narcotic gas, he changed the diagrams on the wall of the room. I believe that he decided he must pretend to be killed himself after he forced me, with drugs, to tell where Kirkpatrick's and my suspicions pointed! That was the real tip-off."

THE SPEEDOMETER needle hovered at seventy-eight. Not all of Jackson's efforts had been able to get it higher. They were blazing up Riverside Drive at last, reaching for the Towers in the middle Eighties. The tires skidded the last thirty feet and Wentworth reeled to the street almost before it stopped. He drew the revolver from his belt, braced himself wide-legged with a hand pressed to his side. Then he put his head down and walked through the open doors.

In the elevator, he said huskily, "Eighth!" Jackson pushed the dumbfounded operator from the elevator and sent it upward himself. He had an automatic in his fist and when the cage stopped, he whipped open the door and went out first. There was a heavy double crash of guns and Jackson pitched face down

from a substitution alphabet in which A equals O, B equals P, C equals Q and so on; that the third letter would be taken from a substitution alphabet in which A equals T. After that, he repeated the sequence of rotating substitution alphabets, and interpreting the code message JCLUC, he obtained ROSCO, the name of the steel company whose president was the next to be murdered by the tit-tat-toe artist. In a similar way, using the first three letters as the key for rotating substitution alphabets, he read the other messages. Herein is the key for the tit-tat-toe cypher.

on the floor of the hall. His uniform cap dribbled along the wall and lay still. There was a hole through its crown.

Wentworth went out of the elevator on braced legs, his eyes burning hotly in his head. He knew which door to look at, and he saw the gun leveled through the peephole. His revolver bucked in his hand and there was a shrill cry.

The Spider's lips twitched. He pushed with painful perseverance toward the door at which he had shot. He pressed the muzzle of the gun to the lock, pulled the trigger twice, and his shoulder opened the door. He had one bullet left.

He stood still while the door clapped shut behind him. Then he moved steadily along a narrow hall at the end of which he could see a lighted room.

He moved a little farther until he could see half of davenport, could see Nita stretched on it with her head lolling back, her hands hanging. About her throat were wrapped the long, limber fingers of the Master of the Plague.

Wentworth took another step and fired. The impact of the lead knocked the killer's grip from Nita's throat and her body slumped down to the floor. Wentworth stood just inside the room, looking at Nita, then looking into the burning eyes of the Master of the Plague. He moved forward, relentlessly.

"Now, butcher, it's time you die!"

The Master did not lack courage. He lifted his right hand so that the scarlet silken sleeve slid back from his wrist, ducked his over-size head and charged with a shrill, harsh scream.

Wentworth's hands moved with a swift, sure strength and gripped the Plague Master's throat.

THE MAN fought terribly. His right fist pounded cruelly at Wentworth's wounded side. He gouged at Wentworth's eyes and kicked at his body.

Blackness roared before the Spider's gaze, swarmed over his brain. But throughout his being there was only one thought, one transcendent purpose—to kill this man. A snarl pushed out of his lips. He wrenched at that neck he gripped as if he would tear head from body, and he realized that he was being forced backward to the wide, opened studio window. The Master of the Plague saw his own death approaching but he would take the Spider with him...!

It was a battle of waning strengths, the Spider against the butcher. Even seconds might doom him now, seconds that might see the end of consciousness. Despair was in his pain-riven soul. Jackson was dead, out there in the hall; Nita strangled....

Wentworth's staring eyes widened as he gazed past the huge, bald head of the Plague Master. For there was Jackson, staggering along the hall, a bloody tear on his scalp marking the course of the bullet. Even as the brave man advanced, Nita stirred faintly on the floor.

A cry like a great cheer rose in Wentworth's throat. He stared into the bulging eyes of the Plague Master and laughed....

With that strange strength of madness and despair, of an exhausted man who suddenly sees hope and help, Wentworth lifted the Master of the Plague bodily from the floor, spun about and flung him through the studio window, down through the dark emptiness of the night to the pavement eight stories below!

Wentworth staggered then, but he managed to reach Nita's

side before he fell upon his knees; managed to see her slow smile as she lifted weary arms to him.

He tried to laugh lightly and didn't know if he had succeeded. "To think that excuse for a man could hope to win you!"

Nita whispered, "Hush, Dick! Don't even think it. But I never guessed, Dick, until he brought me to this apartment, that the Master of the Plague had killed another man disguised as himself—that the Man in Scarlet was... Sam Ralds!"

THE SPIDER

- ❑ #1: The Spider Strikes — $13.95
- ❑ #2: The Wheel of Death — $13.95
- ❑ #3: Wings of the Black Death — $13.95
- ❑ #4: City of Flaming Shadows — $13.95
- ❑ #5: Empire of Doom! — $13.95
- ❑ #6: Citadel of Hell — $13.95
- ❑ #7: The Serpent of Destruction — $13.95
- ❑ #8: The Mad Horde — $13.95
- ❑ #9: Satan's Death Blast — $13.95
- ❑ #10: The Corpse Cargo — $13.95
- ❑ #11: Prince of the Red Looters — $13.95
- ❑ #12: Reign of the Silver Terror — $13.95
- ❑ #13: Builders of the Dark Empire — $13.95
- ❑ #14: Death's Crimson Juggernaut — $13.95
- ❑ #15: The Red Death Rain — $13.95
- ❑ #16: The City Destroyer — $13.95
- ❑ #17: The Pain Emperor — $13.95
- ❑ #18: The Flame Master — $13.95
- ❑ #19: Slaves of the Crime Master — $13.95
- ❑ #20: Reign of the Death Fiddler — $13.95
- ❑ #21: Hordes of the Red Butcher — $13.95
- ❑ #22: Dragon Lord of the Underworld — $13.95
- ❑ #23: Master of the Death-Madness — $13.95
- ❑ #24: King of the Red Killers — $13.95
- ❑ #25: Overlord of the Damned — $13.95
- ❑ #26: Death Reign of the Vampire King — $13.95
- ❑ #27: Emperor of the Yellow Death — $13.95
- ❑ #28: The Mayor of Hell — $13.95
- ❑ #29: Slaves of the Murder Syndicate — $13.95
- ❑ #30: Green Globes of Death — $13.95
- ❑ **NEW:** #31: The Cholera King — $13.95

THE MYSTERIOUS WU FANG

- ❑ #1: The Case of the Six Coffins — $12.95
- ❑ #2: The Case of the Scarlet Feather — $12.95
- ❑ #3: The Case of the Yellow Mask — $12.95
- ❑ #4: The Case of the Suicide Tomb — $12.95
- ❑ #5: The Case of the Green Death — $12.95
- ❑ #6: The Case of the Black Lotus — $12.95
- ❑ #7: The Case of the Hidden Scourge — $12.95

G-8 AND HIS BATTLE ACES

- ❑ #1: The Bat Staffel — $13.95

CAPTAIN SATAN

- ❑ #1: The Mask of the Damned — $13.95
- ❑ #2: Parole for the Dead — $13.95
- ❑ #3: The Dead Man Express — $13.95
- ❑ #4: A Ghost Rides the Dawn — $13.95
- ❑ #5: The Ambassador From Hell — $13.95

THE SECRET 6

- ❑ 1: The Red Shadow — $13.95
- ❑ #2: House of Walking Corpses — $13.95
- ❑ **NEW:** #3: The Monster Murders — $13.95

CAPTAIN ZERO

- ❑ #1: City of Deadly Sleep — $13.95
- ❑ #2: The Mark of Zero! — $13.95
- ❑ #3: The Golden Murder Syndicate — $13.95

OPERATOR 5

- ❑ #1: The Masked Invasion — $13.95
- ❑ #2: The Invisible Empire — $13.95
- ❑ #3: The Yellow Scourge — $13.95
- ❑ #4: The Melting Death — $13.95
- ❑ #5: Cavern of the Damned — $13.95
- ❑ #6: Master of Broken Men — $13.95
- ❑ #7: Invasion of the Dark Legions — $13.95
- ❑ #8: The Green Death Mists — $13.95
- ❑ #9: Legions of Starvation — $13.95
- ❑ #10: The Red Invader — $13.95
- ❑ #11: The League of War-Monsters — $13.95
- ❑ #12: The Army of the Dead — $13.95
- ❑ #13: March of the Flame Marauders — $13.95
- ❑ #14: Blood Reign of the Dictator — $13.95
- ❑ #15: Invasion of the Yellow Warlords — $13.95
- ❑ #16: Legions of the Death Master — $13.95

DUSTY AYRES AND HIS BATTLE BIRDS

- ❑ #1: Black Lightning! — $13.95
- ❑ #2: Crimson Doom — $13.95
- ❑ #3: The Purple Tornado — $13.95
- ❑ #4: The Screaming Eye — $13.95
- ❑ #5: The Green Thunderbolt — $13.95
- ❑ #6: The Red Destroyer — $13.95
- ❑ #7: The White Death — $13.95
- ❑ #8: The Black Avenger — $13.95
- ❑ #9: The Silver Typhoon — $13.95
- ❑ #10: The Troposphere F-S — $13.95
- ❑ #11: The Blue Cyclone — $13.95
- ❑ #12: The Tesla Raiders — $13.95

DR. YEN SIN

- ❑ #1: Mystery of the Dragon's Shadow — $12.95
- ❑ #2: Mystery of the Golden Skull — $12.95
- ❑ #3: Mystery of the Singing Mummies — $12.95

MAVERICKS

- ❑ #1: Five Against the Law — $12.95
- ❑ #2: Mesquite Manhunters — $12.95
- ❑ #3: Bait for the Lobo Pack — $12.95
- ❑ #4: Doc Grimson's Outlaw Posse — $12.95
- ❑ #5: Charlie Parr's Gunsmoke Cure — $12.95